Home for Christmas
A Frost Family Christmas Story

Roxy Boroughs

Publisher: Baucis & Philemon

Cover Designer: Kim Killion at Hot Damn Designs at http://www.hotdamndesigns.com/

Editor: Linda Style at http://www.EditingwithStyle.net and Mr. Ted Williams, Freelance Editor

Layout: WriteAdvice Consulting

Formatting by Anessa Books

ISBN-13: 978-0992127107

ISBN-10: 0992127106

Dedication and Acknowledgements

For Barry, my very own rock star.

Thanks to my fellow Frost Family writers, C. J. Carmichael and Brenda M. Collins. And to my critique partners Lecia Cornwall, Pamela Yaye and Sherile Reilly.

A special thank you to Moira Stelmack for sharing her expertise on autism. Any errors in the story are mine, not hers.

And thanks to Serena Ryder and her hit Stompa, my theme music for this story.

Chapter One

James Frost cracked open the windows of his new Porsche and immediately felt the cold. Not only from the December air, but from the town.

He'd grown up in Carol Falls. Stolen his first kiss here. And run away from the place as fast as he could.

Nestled in the shadow of the Green Mountains near I-89 in Vermont, the town was strategically located between Burlington and Montpelier—distant enough from both spots to bask in its own rural feel, while close enough to the state's largest city and its capital to have all the amenities anyone could want.

But it lacked the person he most desired.

She was gone. *Long gone.*

James crossed the red covered bridge that stretched over the snowy banks of the Carol River, and had second thoughts about heading straight to his family's maple syrup farm.

Unsure of his welcome.

So he cruised around the stomping grounds of his youth—drove by the police station where his sister worked, and then he inspected the new paint job on the town hall, an improvement he'd missed during his last visit to Carol Falls in March. When he reached his old school at the end of the street, he hung a right. Best to avoid White Pine Ridge High.

Heading back in the direction he'd come, he noticed a number of vehicles parked at the end of Aspen Street. Either someone had invited the entire population to a Christmas party, or folks were enjoying the Village Green. Skating on the rink, no doubt.

As he turned the corner and found a vacant slot for his own car, he saw several people on skates gliding over the ice, their boldly striped scarves of red and orange flapping behind them. Others gathered around the huge Balsam fir, decorating it as they did every year. He remembered his parents bringing him here, along with his brother and sister, all of them drinking hot chocolate and waiting for the moment when the sixty-footer would be lit up like...well...

Like a Christmas tree.

Its scent filled the air—a rich, woodsy aroma that embodied the season. It mingled with the smell of hot apple cider, the spicy odor of cloves making James crave a cupful.

A second later, he was cringing at the next song to play over the loudspeakers—Kelly Clarkson's version of *I'll be Home for Christmas*. Not that he had anything against the singer. Just the sentiment. This wasn't his home anymore, merely a business opportunity. Best to keep that point uppermost in his mind.

He left his car, tugged at the collar on his leather jacket and dredged up his courage. As he approached the tree on foot, the crowd parted and a little boy ran to him. The kid's nose was red from the cold and his big grin infectious.

"Uncle Jimmy!"

James' nephew jumped into his arms. The boy's cool, apple cheek pressed against James' warmer one. "How's it going, Dunc?"

"Good. Grandma said you might come to see me. And guess what! We've got a baby at the farm. Isn't that neat?"

Very. James figured one of the barn cats must have had a surprise litter. "A baby kitten?"

"No. A baby *human*. We found it in the manger the night of Frosty Frolics. Somebody left it there. And guess what! We named her Holly, 'cause it's almost Christmas and she's a girl."

What the heck? An abandoned baby left at his parents' farm during their annual winter event? *Typical*. The one year James missed Frosty Frolics, something extraordinary had happened. Before he could question Duncan further, the five-year-old's attention span moved on to other, more pressing issues.

"Can we play hockey? And go tobogganing? Can you teach me a song on the guitar? And—"

"Whoa, buddy. I'm only in town for a week." James tossed his nephew into the air and then caught the giggling bundle. "And what makes you think I brought my guitar?"

More laughter. "Because you always do, silly. So will you teach me?"

James found it difficult to refuse, especially when the child wrapped two skinny arms around his neck and hugged him fiercely.

Duncan could make James forget all the reasons he hated Carol Falls with one squeeze. "I know some three-chord Christmas tunes. We can start with those."

"And you can read to me. I have a bunch of new books..."

The boy listed several titles, but James barely heard him. He was too busy planning a way to avoid story time. He set the wiggling tyke back down on terra firma.

"Lily's been reading Doctor Zeus to me."

"Suess," a pretty, blonde woman corrected. James had seen her approach as he talked to Duncan. And James' brother, Garret, was with her, his arm around her waist.

Chalk one up to their matchmaking mother, James thought. The last time he'd talked to her on the phone, besides pressuring him to visit for Christmas, she'd mentioned a new employee—a gorgeous gal from the Big Apple sure to catch Garret's attention and end his days as a single parent and widower. Judging from the love light in his brother's eyes, their mom had found the perfect mate for her eldest son. The guy was plainly head over heels, and James could see why. The woman radiated an inner beauty that matched her outer appeal, and she was obviously as crazy about Garret as he was about her.

James couldn't help but feel a wee bit jealous. He'd once had a special girl who'd looked at him like that.

"Good to see you, Jimmy," Garret said, clapping him on the back in a mechanical move—the Tin Man in need of oil.

James didn't have to imagine what he, himself, would look like in seven years. People had always said he was a younger version of his big brother. They were both tall, had the same hazel eyes and the same dark hair—although James didn't cut his as often.

"Mom and Dad are at the house. Did you stop there first?"

"No. I saw the crowd here. Thought I'd check it out."

"And now they're checking out your car." Garret used his nose to point out the swarm of love-sick auto enthusiasts buzzing around the vehicle. "That's quite the ride, Jimbo. Did you rob a bank?"

Garret and the blonde chuckled. So did James, though the question felt like sandpaper against the grain of his ego. Jokes often revealed the truth. Did a part of Garret believe James didn't have the wherewithal to earn a nice ride on his own?

Driving here in the Porsche had seemed like such a good idea when he was back in Boston. His boss, Stephen Harker, loved the car and owned one just like it. Only in blue. James chose red for his. *Showier.* Now a wave of heat crawled up his neck, despite the chill and the flakes of snow that whirled around him. He'd thought the fancy vehicle would help him feel like a big man strutting back to prove to everyone how wrong they were about him. He should have taken his truck, instead. It would have been more practical on the snowy roads, and he would have felt less like a jerk now for trying too hard to impress.

"This is Lily Parker," Garret went on, introducing the blonde. "She's the PR manager Mom hired for the farm."

"Glad to meet you, Jimmy."

"James," he said, shaking Lily's outstretched hand. "And likewise."

"I have to admit, I've been rather curious about you," she said. "Garret tells me you don't make it home very often."

"Last time was in the....*spring.* Right, Jimbo?"

Another sentence Garret packed with hidden meaning. And disapproval. James supposed he deserved it after his behavior during *that* visit to Carol Falls. He strove for good-natured indifference with his responding, "Uh-huh," and ignored the bait. For Lily's sake. It wasn't her fault he and Garret had a history.

And speaking of history...

James stared past them. For a few seconds, his heart forgot to beat. Over by the tree stood someone he'd never thought he'd meet again. Not in this life.

They'd barely reached seventeen when he'd last seen her, when he'd last kissed her, when he'd slipped a simple, gold band on her finger.

Even with dusk approaching, she lit up the park—the sun-kissed strands of her caramel-colored hair catching the remaining light. Her creamy skin looked so touchable he had to fist his hands to control himself. Was it possible she'd grown more beautiful in the past ten years?

He'd been with other women since they'd parted. No one had ever come close to her in his life. He'd been accused, more than once, of encasing his feelings in armor. And maybe he had. But no woman had ever broken through his protective shield like April.

Only to break him with her rejection.

No sooner had the thought come to him than he noticed April

adjusting the hat of a young boy who looked about ten. The action was so maternal—the way she smiled at the child, the gentle quality of her movements. Was the boy her son?

The breath froze in his lungs as he watched his ex gently turn the kid to face the tree. The lad seemed distant, no more interested in the decorating than James had been in school.

He did the math. The girl who'd promised to love him forever, the one he'd spent most of his adult life pining over, must have moved on from him and immediately created a family with another man.

Merry Christmas.

It was enough to make him get in his car and head back to Boston. But he had business to attend to. Business that would set Vermont on its ear and show the naysayers, and his lost love, that James Frost had finally made something of himself.

A scattered countdown began, the crowd doing their ten-nine-eight shtick in anticipation of the official lighting. With each number, more voices chimed in—Lily, Garret and Duncan adding to the volume. While everyone else focused on the tree, April's little boy looked at the ground. He twirled on the spot, flapping his arms like a baby bird.

"Three...two...one!"

The tree burst into color, thousands of lights glittering from its boughs, reminding James of a starry sky on a clear night in the country. The town folk *ooh*ed and *aah*ed, but the boy near April didn't notice. He continued to flutter his arms and spin until James got dizzy watching him.

Distantly, he heard Lily's voice. "That's April Rochester. Her son is autistic, poor kid."

James nodded, though he didn't really know what that meant. *Autistic?* It seemed as if the boy was locked in his own world. An outsider. Someone who didn't fit in.

And James knew exactly how that felt.

"Marcus."

Sometimes, if April called her son's name, she could get him to focus.

Not usually, though. Hardly ever, really, but she was grasping for any way to break through.

She could see he was over stimulated. The spinning and flapping were simply ways for him to cope with the sensory overload. Had she rushed him? Brought him to Carol Falls too fast? Exposed him to their new neighbors too soon?

She bent forward and retied his scarf. He didn't acknowledge her, just stared at some unknown thing out of the corner of his eye.

"Marcus, please look at me."

If anything, he'd reverted into himself after the move. Understandable. His disorder craved routine, sameness. Still, the change had been necessary. Finances demanded it.

All she could do was give him a hug. Some autistic children hated to be touched, others found deep compression comforting. Marcus was in the latter group, so she wrapped him up in her arms and held him tight, wondering if there would ever come a day when he would return her embrace.

If he would ever call her Mommy.

"Marcus..."

The boy's gaze drifted back to hers, but failed to connect. The festivities were obviously too much for him. Time to go home.

Or at least to her late grandfather's maple syrup farm. That was home now.

She felt a tug and looked down, expecting to find Marcus pulling on her coat to get her attention. But he wasn't. The sensation persisted and she shrugged it off. When she straightened and turned to leave, a vision from her past stood before her, looking every bit as good—*no*, better—than she remembered.

"Jimmy."

The shock of seeing him again made her knees weak. Or was that from his closeness? She would have known him anywhere, though a decade had passed since she'd last seen him, and he'd filled out in the most mouth-watering ways. He was broader in the shoulders and chest, but remained slim in the hips. He still wore his hair on the longish side, and his eyes smoldered as they used to, her skin heating wherever his glance touched.

Now she understood that pull she'd felt. She'd always been able to tell when Jimmy was nearby. At school, if he walked into the cafeteria, she knew he was there before she saw him. Felt his presence, as if they were attached by some unseen thread. It tugged at her still, drawing her in, though his current expression was shuttered.

"April...I didn't expect to see you here."

She wished she'd worn something nicer, put on some lip gloss—*heck*, stopped to brush her hair. "I just moved back to town." Goodness, was that breathy, girlish voice coming out of her mouth? "My grandfather left me his old house on the highway. You know the place."

Of course, he did. At sixteen, they'd both spent time on the adjoining farm. Late winter saw them helping with the harvest. By summer, they were kissing under the leafy umbrella of the maple trees, love blooming amongst the wildflowers.

Jimmy's eyes narrowed. "I'll have to check it out when I'm on the interstate. I've been asked to assess several parcels of land on I-89 for a business venture."

Business? She'd pictured him as a rock star and imagined him involved in the music industry. Maybe as a composer, churning out hit songs. Or producing them. Certainly not evaluating land for a business, unless it was a recording studio. And why build one in Boondocks, Vermont?

"Are you in town for awhile? Staying with the family?" She'd heard he'd left home long ago and returned infrequently, and only for big family functions, like Christmas and funerals.

"For a week. Or until they throw me out," he answered—half-funny, half-serious.

"I'm sure you're safe." In her peripheral vision, she caught Marcus spinning again. She grasped his hand and drew him to her. "Jimmy, this is my..."

She always introduced Marcus as her son, although he'd actually been hers for only two months. Why did she hesitate now?

"...my son, Marcus. Marcus, this is Jimmy, an old..."

Golly, anyone would think she was the one with communication problems instead of her boy. What was she supposed to call the man she'd once been married to for a full twenty minutes?

"Jimmy's an old friend of mine." She smoothed the hair away from Marcus' eyes, but he didn't bother to lift his head. For him, April's adolescent crush ranked right up there with the Invisible Man.

"It's James now," her former sweetheart announced.

"James," she repeated. It sounded as foreign on her tongue as it had on his. The way he looked at her was foreign too, with a stony detachment that startled her. The playfulness they used to share was gone.

She had to put away her schoolgirl fantasies about him. He was older now. He probably had a wife and children of his own. She wished he'd take his hands out of his pockets so she could see if he wore a ring. Not all men did, but the Jimmy she'd known would have worn it proudly. He'd often said all he wanted in life was to marry and have kids.

With her.

Those were long ago days, never to be recaptured.

She'd written to him after their breakup, explaining everything. He never replied, never contacted her. Had he destroyed the note unread? Would she be a fool to ask about it now and face another brush off? Feel its bite?

Definitely.

At her side, Marcus started flapping again with his one, free arm. "Sorry, but we should get going. It's been a long day for my son."

Jimmy gave himself a small shake, as if coming out of a trance. "Certainly." He stood aside to let her pass.

And that was it, the end of their reunion. April returned his guarded smile, took a step, and then felt his hand on her arm—melting her on the spot, throwing her off balance.

"It was nice seeing you again, April."

Her brain scrambled. For a few seconds, every thought flew out of her head, replaced by the awareness of his touch. When his hand (his right one, darn it) returned to his side, her gray matter aligned and she regained her footing.

"You, too."

She walked away on wobbly legs, wondering if the rush she'd just experienced was real or if sleep deprivation had finally turned her mind to mush. Must have, given the fantasies playing up there.

She was a parent now. To a special needs child. She didn't have the energy to mother Jimmy, as well. Not like she'd done in high school. Making sure he showed up on time and typing the book reports he dictated to her—*after* she'd summarized the plots for him, of course. Because he was *soooo* busy with sports he couldn't bother reading a bunch of stupid novels written by dead, white guys.

His rebellious line, not hers.

And, back in the day, that bad boy attitude gave her palpitations. Nonsense she couldn't afford now.

After she found her SUV and made sure Marcus was buckled up, she clutched her good luck charm—the one that dangled from a plain, gold chain around her neck.

Was she crazy to wear it? To believe in fate?

She'd often dreamed of seeing Jimmy again. Never had the meeting in her imagination been so one-sided, with her lovesick and him disinterested. Hoping for something to happen between them was a lost cause. One she should have abandoned long ago.

April glanced back at the tree, at the star shining from its very top and made her wish—that she could forget about Jimmy as easily as he appeared to have forgotten about her.

Chapter Two

James spent an uncomfortable night in his childhood bedroom where, until recently, his nephew had slept.

After Duncan's mother died, a little over two years ago, Garret thought it best to move back into the family home with his son. Now that Lily had come into Garret's life, and helped him conquer his remaining grief, James' big brother and Duncan were happily ensconced in their own house again, located on the other side of the farm.

Unfortunately, not all of Dunc's toys had gone with him. Partway through the night, a plastic dinosaur, hiding in the jungle of covers, tried to take a chunk out of James' side.

His discomfort, however, had more to do with thoughts of April than prehistoric critters, and late night dreams about how their lives could have been different if they'd only stayed together.

Namely, Marcus would have been *his* son and not another man's.

James scrubbed a hand over his face. Who was he fooling? He wouldn't have been ready for parenthood a decade ago. Particularly, to a child who needed extra attention. He'd just grown up himself in the last few years.

Thanks to Stephen Harker.

They'd met when the CEO hired James as a private contractor to build an addition on his house. The two hit it off instantly and, after the work was done, James became Harker's regular go-to guy. If Stephen wanted a second opinion on a parcel of land for a new Getalot store, he called James. Once the location was set, James became the supervisor on site, monitoring every aspect of the build. The big boss went so far as to provide James with a secretary, who did all the dull parts of the job, like type up schedules and contracts.

Who could ask for a better gig?

James yanked the baseball-themed comforter up to his chin and slipped out of bed, his trick to avoid the fuss of making it. He smoothed the wrinkles with one stroke of his hand and called the job done. He'd heard the sound of the shower running earlier but it was quiet now, so he grabbed his kit and trotted down the hall to the bathroom, where he washed and dressed.

Retrieving his cell phone and jacket from the bedroom, he paused to look out the window—his favorite spot in the house. He loved the view of the farm from this angle and his sports trophies were still displayed on a lone shelf above the curtain rod.

He liked the window for another reason. As a kid, he'd found a loose floorboard under the carpet just below it. The space between two joists formed a rectangular cubbyhole he used for stashing his treasures: an eagle feather, a silver dollar and a special collection of picks featuring his guitar heroes—Eric Clapton, Jimi Hendrix, Neil Young and B. B. King.

During his first long trip away from home, his mother had inadvertently turned his secret compartment into a time capsule, when she'd brought in a contractor to rip up all the carpeting and replace it with hardwood. Her actions sealed in James' keepsakes and marked the beginning of his interest in home repair and construction. He'd wanted to learn how to rip out that patch of flooring and replace it without his mom knowing.

The timing for the excavation never seemed right though, and he'd forgotten about his secret hiding place. Until he saw April again. She brought back all those memories. And regrets over what might have been.

If James hadn't known his way to the kitchen, the smell of coffee would have led him there. He nixed using the banister on his way down the stairs because of the scratchy garland looped around it. He heard someone humming in the living room and spotted his mother's housekeeper wiping the mantel, re-hanging the family's Christmas stockings as she went. She wore loose-fitting, navy blue hospital scrubs, a standard uniform that had inspired James to privately dub her The Doctor of Dust.

"How's it going, Mrs. Belmont?"

"Hi, Jimmy. Your mom is so excited you're home." Though Verna's voice was upbeat, she looked tired, older than her forty-odd years.

"Your daughter, Ivy, is—what—fifteen now?"

"Sixteen. And such a help to me with the other children."

If he remembered correctly, Mrs. Belmont and her husband had four or five. A big, happy family. "Clients must keep you hopping this time of year with all the Christmas parties."

"I've been very lucky. Your mother's given me extra hours, too...now that she's busy with baby Holly."

"And that's just the little lady I want to meet. I only got a peek at her last night."

"She's in the kitchen with your mom."

James thanked Verna and followed the wood-paneled hall to the rear of the house. Like practically every other room under this roof, he found his mother had decorated the kitchen for the holidays, too. There was a live poinsettia on the window ledge, and embroidered ones on the dish towel and oven mitts hanging near the stove.

The cooking area formed a U-shape along one end of the kitchen. Black countertops accented the light yellow walls and cabinets, and a host of preserves and spices graced the shelves. A snowman cookie jar stood sentinel, watching over his mother's prized Blue Willow serving platters. These were safely out of Duncan's reach, to prevent breakage and before-dinner-snacking. Opposite all this stood a large oak table, with the morning paper and baby paraphernalia strewn across its top.

His mom sat in one of the kitchen chairs, silvery waves framing her face. She had Holly cradled with one hand, a bottle poised for feeding in the other. She cooed at the tiny girl and received a yawn in return.

James reached over and stroked the dimpled skin along the infant's knuckles and, for a moment, imagined himself as a father. Her tiny hand wrapped around his index finger and held on tight. "She's beautiful. And strong. A little angel."

"Not at night, she isn't. You're lucky your room is at the other end of the house."

He hadn't thought so as a kid. He'd assumed his family stuck him in that bedroom to keep him out of their way. Once he reached his teens, however, he'd loved the privacy, knowing he could stay up late and practice his guitar, a Christmas gift from his doting grandmother that he'd learned to play by ear.

That secluded room had come in handy again it seemed, this time to buffer him from the baby's cries. In spite of his mom's complaint, James had never seen her so energized, her eyes as bright and shiny as the copper kettle on the stove.

"If you hold Holly, I can fix you some eggs," she offered.

James willingly took the little girl from his mom, but *ixnayed* the breakfast. "That's okay. You're busy and I should get a move on." He rocked the child in his arms, the sweet smell of baby powder tickling his nose.

His mother frowned. "You're not leaving already."

James couldn't fault her assumption. The last time he'd come to town, he'd stayed two nights, but only one under his parents' roof. It was natural for her to think he'd bail so quickly.

He kissed her forehead. "I'll be around for a week, or so."

"I'd hoped you'd stay for Christmas."

Guilt niggled at him. He shrugged it away. "I've got things to do, Mom."

"There's lots to do right here, Jimmy. Garret could sure use your help with the farm."

No thanks! James had no intention of letting his big brother boss him around. Any more than usual.

When their dad retired, Garret took over the family business. And rightly so. Garret loved the farm, had devoted himself to it. There was no room for James.

Oh sure, they would have made a spot for him. They were his folks, after all. But he'd spent enough time living in Garret's shadow, and James couldn't bear to see his parents' disappointment every time he let them down.

"Farming's not for me, Mom."

"But, honey, you always had such a green thumb. When you weren't using it to strum on your guitar."

Was she thinking about the mess he'd made of his father's birthday party in the spring?

"I'm going out for a while," he announced, returning the baby to his mother. "On business."

"What are you up to, Jimmy? And how did you come by that fancy car of yours?"

His chest swelled with pride. "Guess you saw it parked out front. Did Dad?"

"Yes, after we heard all about it from Garret. Did you win the lottery, or something?"

Not his mom, too. "No. I've got a steady client who pays me

really well."

"Tell me about him."

"Soon. You'll hear all about it, soon." Once the new Getalot store opened in Vermont, everyone would know about his success. And, frankly, he'd rather they discovered it that way. He wasn't keeping it a secret. Not exactly. He just found it difficult to talk about the job with his folks.

"After you tell me how you ended up with this little bundle," he prompted, referring to baby Holly again.

"We found her in the manger of our nativity set the night of Frosty Frolics. I'm sure the mother, whoever she is, knew that we've taken in foster kids on occasion. It's obvious the poor woman wanted the child cared for but, unfortunately, isn't in a position to do that herself."

"Maybe a teen who got in the family way and couldn't tell anyone?"

"Very likely. Though she had the presence of mind to drop off supplies with the newborn—diapers and formula. The police contacted Helen Kirkwood at family services, who did the paperwork to arrange for temporary foster care, so the baby is able to stay here for now."

"What about later?"

His mother sighed. "I really don't know. We're assuming Holly is from the community so we'd like to see her remain in Carol Falls. It's not your sister's case but maybe she can figure out a way to make it happen."

As in *pull some strings*? That sounded about right when it came to Josephine. James didn't have a whole lot in common with his younger sister, except for a tendency to bend the rules. Joey always seemed to get away with it, though. Maybe that was because with James, bending generally led to breaking.

"I'm going to head into town, Mom."

"Your dad is cooking our usual Sunday dinner. You'll be here for it, right?"

The weekend beef roast was a family tradition and one of James' favorite meals. Generally, his dad cooked the meat and everyone else chipped in with the side dishes. James was an old hand at preparing vegetables, just not fussy about eating them. He was looking forward to some of his mom's homemade horseradish, though. The talk around the table could get almost as heated as the potent condiment. James wondered who'd dig into him the most this evening, his father or Garret.

"Don't worry. I'll be back to help you with the veggies, Mom."

He took a step to leave but she clutched his hand. "It's good to see you, Jimmy. I wish you'd visit more often. And stay for Christmas."

He smiled at her and she nodded, as if she already realized that her wish was impossible. Parents have favorites. They try not to, but it happens. Maybe you're closer to the kid who's most like you. Maybe you can't stand him for the same reason, because that child reminds you too much of yourself. However it worked, James knew he and his mom shared a special connection that stemmed from a mutual love of music and sports. His father, meanwhile, favored Garret. And Joey had always been Daddy's little girl. So where did that leave James' mother when he wasn't around?

He gave her another kiss to help even the score, and headed out.

As he brushed the flakes from his car, he heard a rustling. He looked in the direction of the sound and spotted a large, black dog— its nose in the snow, foraging. It didn't appear to have a collar but, at this distance, James couldn't tell for sure. He whistled and the dog's head jerked up, revealing a white patch of fur on its chest.

"Hey, pal. You lost?"

As much as James wanted to help the animal, he knew approaching it was a bad idea. The dog didn't act sick, or wild, but either could be a possibility. He crouched down to its level and slapped his palm against his thigh. "Here, pal."

Its tail waved back and forth—an enthusiastic *hello*—as the dog bounded toward James. Halfway across the yard, the animal slammed on its brakes, ears cocked. A second later, it veered off, engaged in the high speed pursuit of a squirrel.

"Good luck with that," James hollered after the mutt, before it disappeared from sight. He poked his head back into the house long enough to warn his mother about the stray. He didn't want to take any chances with his young nephew's safety.

Satisfied he'd done all he could about the dog situation for the moment, he started his car and drove down Maple Farm Road, noting the mayor's McMansion as he passed it. Even in the morning sun, the place was lit up with so many flashing lights you'd think the owner was advertising a Broadway premiere. James sure didn't envy the cock-of-the-walk, Emerson Lincoln, his electric bill.

The covered bridge came up fast on his right. He could easily cross it and take the next turn to April's house. He was considering land in the area, after all, but he might make trouble for her if he went knocking on her door. Especially if a guy answered.

She still went by her maiden name—Rochester—but that didn't mean much these days. She could be married, divorced, or living common law. James doubted many men would appreciate their significant other's old flame showing up unannounced. Or buy the explanation that James happened to be in the neighborhood. April's farm was the only thing on that road.

So he turned left toward the main square, focused on another destination—Kate's Kitchen. All the locals went there. If he wanted to get the vibe on public opinion, and find out if people were keen on having a Getalot store in northern Vermont, Kate's was a great place to start.

He parked in front of the cafe—a two-story, red brick structure. Green shutters framed the apartment windows on the top floor while, at street level, two white bay windows jutted out toward the sidewalk, the entrance of the cafe sandwiched neatly between them. Like every other business in town, Christmas was energetically heralded at Kate's. Huge festive wreaths hung in the windows and boughs of holly burst from the accompanying flowerboxes.

As James walked into the eating establishment, two things hit him—the familiar jingle of the bells on the door and the heavenly aroma of cinnamon and apples. He inhaled his fill as he scanned the eclectic selection of wooden tables and chairs that made up the decor. Instead of looking disorganized, the mismatched furnishings gave the place a homey feel, as if you were visiting a dear friend who'd managed to borrow an extra seat from a neighbor, just so you'd have a comfy place to roost.

On the walls were photos of Kate's travels, shots of the places and people she'd met during her first career as a journalist. There was a photo of Kate at the Great Wall of China, large color prints of her shaking hands with celebrities, even one of her posing with members of the royal family in England. These were in marked contrast to the lighthearted Christmas decorations inside the cafe, the most whimsical of which was a hip-high toy moose presiding over the cash register, while wearing a pair of striped elf socks to warm his antlers.

James had, unfortunately, missed the morning rush. There were few people for him to question but, on the upside, he had his choice of tables. He sat in a big captain's chair and picked up a discarded newspaper. His reading skills had improved since high school but it was still a slog. Small case Ds and Bs continued to trip him up and sounding out a long word was murder, but he kept at it, practicing when he had a chance.

Kate Wedge, herself, jogged over to him, pad and paper in hand, her thick ponytail swinging. "Well, well. Look what the snow blew in. Good to see you, Jimmy."

He stood and returned her affectionate embrace. She was a striking woman—with big, green eyes and beautiful hair. But he'd never wanted to run his fingers through the auburn strands. He knew she was thirty-something—and he'd dated his share of older women—but there'd never been so much as a spark between him and Kate. Whereas, with April, he'd felt like a piece of dry kindling in the middle of a bonfire.

"You know I'd go out of my way for that honeyed smile of yours."

"Flattery will get *you* everything, Prince Charming. Including a piece of pie on the house. Now, what's your pleasure? Coffee? Cream, no sugar?"

She'd remembered. That warmed him more than her java ever could. "And I guess I'll have pancakes with blueberries."

A sigh and an eye roll followed his order. "You ask for that every time you come in. Try something different for a change. Menu's right up there." She gestured to the blackboard above the counter.

James squinted at the list, watching as the printed lines floated together. It always took him a while to decipher text and, under pressure, he generally bailed. The longer he kept someone waiting while he struggled, the more likely they'd be to discover his problem. And he'd spent his life coming up with clever ways to conceal it. Even from his family.

He gave Kate his winning smile and exercised one of his usual escapes. "What do you recommend?"

"My newest dish is a breakfast burrito. You can have it with sausage or bacon."

"Sausage, please."

She winked at him and scooted behind the counter, reappearing moments later with his coffee. As he sipped, he thumbed through the newspaper, while eavesdropping on the locals. Everyone was talking about the abandoned baby. More than a week had passed and no one knew who the kid's parents were.

He also learned there'd been some public mischief in the area. The latest incident saw the town plastered with homemade posters depicting local officials sporting drawn-on mustaches and dunce caps. James remembered a time when nothing happened in sleepy Carol Falls.

A tall woman with long yellow hair, who looked vaguely familiar, brought him a refill along with his burrito, which came with buttery, sourdough toast and a pile of home fries. True to Kate's word, a slice of cherry pie appeared, too.

After he thanked the waitress, she remained hovering at his side, until Kate slid into the empty chair across from him with her own cup of brew. The yellow-haired server gave him a weak smile and continued her rounds with the coffeepot.

"How goes the local economy, Kate?" She'd returned to town about a year ago and opened this business, which was doing gangbusters, judging from the overflowing tip jar at the till.

"For me? Great. I just hired a new server. She's helping with the brunch crowds on Sundays and the weekday morning rush. But there are families hurting for work—like the Smiths, the Browns and the Belmonts. Verna cleans here...for your mom, too, I think." Kate leaned in and whispered, "But her husband, Oliver, isn't pulling his weight. He lost his position with the town a while back due to budget constraints and then started drinking. Your brother gave him a job but Ollie couldn't manage to stay sober and Garret had to let him go. Hopefully soon, Belmont will stop drowning his sorrows and get off his butt."

James hoped so, too. Verna was a good person. She deserved better. And so did their children.

The mound of food on his plate highlighted the inequity between the *Haves* and the *Have-Nots*. James held his fork suspended over his breakfast, shy about digging in after hearing the troubles faced by the less fortunate in the community. A Getalot store would create the jobs those people desperately needed. "Want to share?"

"Heavens, no. I had one of those about an hour ago and I'm still stuffed. You made a good choice...in spite of me having to twist your arm."

James took a bite and agreed. "When I'm working, I usually grab something at Getalot. All the locations have a fast-food restaurant right inside the store, so it's convenient."

"It wouldn't be for me. I'm sure I'd lose business to them if there were a location nearby. For some, a cheap meal wins out over a healthy choice."

At least he knew where Kate stood on the Getalot issue. "So tell me all about this abandoned baby."

"It's still making the front page." Kate patted the newspaper. "The entire story is recapped right here."

And he'd know every detail, if he'd read that far. "I was looking for your personal take. Any idea who might have left their newborn in a manger?"

"None. Erik has been drilling for clues and coming up dry." Kate's younger sibling was a police officer in Carol Falls, something James and the cafe owner had in common.

"It's quite the mystery," she went on, while he ate. "And I used to love covering those kinds of stories back in my days as a reporter. I wish I were clairvoyant like that Long Island psychic on TV. I'd be able to find the parents in a New York minute. I just thank the stars above that the child was left in the care of your family. You hear about babies thrown in garbage cans, as if they're trash. I don't know what's wrong with some people."

"Ditto."

An *ahem* interrupted their exchange. James glanced up to find the leggy waitress again, her lips quivering as she smiled, as if unsure of herself.

"Jimmy, this is my new hire, Heather Connolly."

He stuck out his hand to shake hers. "James. James Frost."

The skin around the blonde's brows crinkled slightly, an almost imperceptible wince. Her smile grew more tremulous. "We've already met, James," she murmured as she pumped his arm.

From her reaction, he could tell he'd hurt her feelings. He hadn't remembered her and that had to sting. "I thought I recognized you but...from where?"

Usually, he was good with faces, but hers was like a cubist

painting—broken up, fragmented. The deep blue of her eyes rang a bell, but the sadness in them didn't. Her jaw line wasn't quite the same as the girl he had in mind, either, and this one carried an extra twenty pounds, or so, around her middle.

"I waitress at Billy Boy's, too. You came into the bar several months ago after..."

His father's sixtieth birthday party.

So she *was* the girl he recalled. Man, you'd have thought he'd outgrown blushing. No chance. The heat spread through his cheeks and down his neck.

That day in March, his sister had this great plan that each of them would write their fondest memory of the old man and surprise him with their readings. Only James had no ability to fill up a page with words. He'd sat stewing while Garret and Joey recited their happy childhood stories, and then everyone looked at him.

He'd reached for his guitar and improvised a song. They seemed to enjoy it, but when he found out his mother had arranged to immortalize each tale in one of her scrapbooking projects, he'd choked on his slice of birthday cake.

He couldn't put the song on paper. His penmanship wasn't a hell of a lot better than Duncan's. He'd watched as his mom merrily glued the other two essays into the book, leaving a couple of blank sheets in between for his contribution. But James knew his hasty input would be a garbled disaster.

Disgusted with himself, he'd made an excuse about needing to run out and buy music paper, but he'd gone to Billy Boy's instead. He drank too much and ended up crashing on Heather's couch. James woke the next morning, swallowed some aspirins to lessen the pounding in his head, and beat it out of town before his mother could ask for those pages again.

Damn. He was no different than Mr. Belmont.

At least he'd followed up and mailed the song to his mom later, after he'd had someone give it a thorough proofing.

"Nice to see you," he said, cutting Heather off so she couldn't elaborate. Though *nice* was hardly the right word. Meeting her again had him reliving a past he wanted to forget. It was like seeing a ghost.

She'd obviously been through some tough times since they'd last met, and he felt sorry for her but, after her reminder of that night, he had only one thought.

To flee.

He stood and reached for his jacket. "I should get going. But it was great seeing you both." James pulled out his wallet. Kate motioned for him to put it back in his pocket.

"Take me out for a glass of wine sometime, and we'll call it even."

With thoughts of that March binge pinging around his head, alcohol was the last thing on his mind. "Thanks."

He left a sizable tip for Heather and flipped up his collar in readiness to step into the cold. Footsteps followed him, and then Kate's voice.

"Did you know April Rochester is back in town?"

"Yeah," he said, buttoning his jacket. "I saw her last night at the tree trimming."

"Any plans to stop by her place?"

"Nope." Not really. Okay, maybe he'd thought about taking a gander when he drove by looking for real estate opportunities. The last thing he needed was to run into the guy who'd claimed her heart. And kept it.

"She's up to her neck, Jimmy," Kate told him, her voice low. "The farm's in bad shape and she's got a special needs child to take care of. She could really use a hand."

His feet were already moving—the urge to run out and help April so strong his body was taking him there before his brain caught up. Fortunately, it remembered the exact moment when she'd ended their relationship, and the resulting ache in his chest.

He held his ground. "What's that to me?"

"I've offered. Others have, too. But she's stubborn. Says she's used to taking care of herself."

"Doesn't she have a..." He swallowed, and forced himself to say the words. "A *husband* to help her?" When he'd last seen April, thick mittens encased her hands. He couldn't check for a wedding ring— one she'd swapped for the band he'd given her.

"She's all alone out there, Jimmy. And with how close the two of you were, I'm sure she'd accept help from you.

Close? He used to think so. Until it came to making their short-lived marriage work. Close hadn't counted then. And it didn't count now.

Chapter Three

Smart people take their own advice. Sadly, James had never been smart. Like a homing pigeon, he flew over the covered bridge and up Tamarack Tree Lane to April's place.

The sun burst through the cloud cover, warming the day. He opened his car window halfway and inhaled. As much as he loved living in the city, the mountain air here was sweet and clean, as intoxicating as a woman's perfume.

He kept thinking about what Kate had said—that April was out here alone. In other words, there was no guy with her. If she'd been married, things hadn't worked out. He felt both bad and glad about the news. Bad for April, glad for himself.

Okay, not exactly glad. *Vindicated* would be a better word. She'd replaced him in a heartbeat, while he'd wasted months pining for her, spending lonely nights feeling sad and bitter. He simply wished she could have trusted in him. In their union.

Not that there was a chance for them to be together now. What they'd shared happened a long time ago. A repeat performance would end the same way, and put him on the losing side.

He pulled off to the shoulder of the road and surveyed April's house and barn. James couldn't believe the changes. Her grandfather built the home seventy years ago and the place showed every bit of its age. The front porch slanted like the steps in an amusement park funhouse. The roof needed work. *Big time*. Some shingles were missing, revealing the underlay. In other spots, he could see right through to the wooden sheathing. A coat of paint might have spruced up the general exterior but, with so many other problems, it would be a waste of money.

Still, the land was good. Especially from an investor's point of view. Situated near the junction of two highways, the location was ideal for a Getalot store. Too bad it wasn't one of the properties Stephen was considering. He could buy the land cheap, April would have money in the bank, and the new retailer could supply jobs for the suffering folks in Carol Falls, while catering to the buying needs of the local communities and tourists. A win-win-win.

James nosed his car into the long driveway and parked. As he walked down the cracked sidewalk, movement caught his eye. Close to the house, on the other side of the peeling picket fence, April's snowsuit-clad son was busy with his toys—a toboggan, a pintsized snow shovel, a green bucket and a plastic Superman chair. The boy seemed like an average kid, until James took a second look. Marcus wasn't actually 'playing' with his toys. He was lining them up. Meticulously.

"Hi, Marcus."

The child didn't acknowledge him, just went right on placing his things in a row, howling in aggravation each time the shovel he'd stuck in the snow fell over.

"Jimmy...if you're planning to play outside with us, you're gonna need a hat."

He'd been so intrigued with Marcus, he hadn't noticed April's approach. "Considering the time of year, maybe I should get one like Santa's," he replied.

Her hat was a teal knit, the same color as her car-length coat. The material almost matched the shade of her eyes. He'd often gazed at her, trying to decide if they were blue or green. Depending on what she wore, and her mood, her eyes seemed to change—blue if she was overtired, green if she was excited.

Always green after a thorough kissing.

He heard a hiss and snapped out of it. At his feet, a well-fed black and white cat stared up at him, indignant. A dark mask of fur ran around the feline's eyes, making him look like a chubby Zorro.

"Don't mind Bandit. He's kind of territorial."

"Ya think?"

Bandit batted the air with his paw, clearly a challenge for James to put up his dukes and fight it out. *Mano-a-mano.*

Weird. Animals usually liked him. Kids, too. James felt like Tiger Woods at the 2013 U.S. Open. Completely off his game.

He glanced over at Marcus again, who was now making snowballs. Instead of throwing them, he was stacking the balls one on top of the other like a mile-high ice cream cone, shouting his frustration whenever they fell over.

"It's good that he can play outside here. It's quiet enough, not a lot of traffic. Kids like Marcus have a tendency to run out into the street, because they're unaware of the danger."

Normally, James wouldn't have asked, but she'd opened the door on the subject. "I've heard he's autistic. What is that, exactly?"

"It's a developmental disorder." She smoothed a strand of hair from her face and looked at her son with a mix of love and worry. "It affects his ability to communicate and interact socially."

"So, the other day, when he was flapping his arms and—"

"It's called stimming, short for self-stimulation. It helps him cope with the world when there are too many sights and sounds for him to process."

James noticed the dark smudges under her eyes. "And how do *you* cope?"

She let out a breath. The chilly vapors surrounded her face like a wreath. "Sometimes, I feel as isolated in the world as he must. But it's what I signed up for. I trained as a teacher for special needs kids, so I'm able to home school him and coach him with his developmental skills. I get discouraged now and then, but I forget all about the downside when I see him make a breakthrough."

She licked her lips, drawing James' attention to them all the more. He could still remember kissing her. She'd tasted like cherry bubblegum, smelled of shampoo, and the sight of her pulse beating madly at the base of her neck used to be enough to drive him over the edge.

He cleared his throat. Unfortunately, it did nothing to clear his head. "Where's the boy's father?" He shouldn't ask, but couldn't stop himself. A part of him wanted to see the guy pull his weight. A bigger part wanted the guy out of the picture entirely. For selfish reasons.

All of which involved April and that luscious mouth.

James' expression turned hard, possessive. And that hungry look in his eyes set April's heart kicking against her ribs with the fervor of a wild bronco.

Where was the boy's father? "I don't know," she answered truthfully. "I never met the man. Or the woman who gave birth to Marcus."

James was quiet for a moment, and then his brows shot up. "He's adopted?"

"Yup. I'm a single mom."

"That's great." His quick smile faded. "I mean, it's great you're giving a home to a kid who needs one. But doing it all on your own—that must be rough."

So was his jaw, dusted with the right amount of stubble to give him an air of danger. She wanted to reach up and touch his cheek, let that roughness caress her palm. Was she crazy to feel this attraction to him after all these years?

Whatever he'd done to send her teenage endorphins skyrocketing tripled now that he was a man. And that spiced-up cologne he wore? She wanted to bury her face against his neck and breathe him in for the next half hour.

"I manage," she said, took a step back and grabbed hold of one of the fence slats—something solid to remind her about the differences between reality and fantasy. The wood was reality. Marcus was reality. Making this month's credit card payment was a *harsh* reality.

Jimmy was a fantasy, her emotions clouded by the memory of the boy she'd once loved. They'd both changed, she was sure of it. She certainly had. Sudden motherhood did that to a girl.

Besides, Jimmy had been the one to reject her in the end.

"So what brings you to my place?"

"I'm doing some legwork in the area for a client. Thought I'd stop by and say hello." He toed a chunk of crusty snow, pulverizing it with this boot. "How 'bout you? What do your folks think about you moving back to Carol Falls?"

The question threw her. If he asked that, he couldn't have read her letter, the tear-stained note she'd churned out explaining her parents' accident.

"They...died."

There was no way he could have faked his shocked expression. His face went slack for a few seconds, his color momentarily drained. "I'm sorry. I didn't know."

She'd been devastated by their deaths, unable to do anything at first except meet with lawyers and arrange a funeral. As an only child, she'd often felt lonely, but never with as much intensity as in those early days of grief. After she recovered from the shock and started planning her new life, she wrote to Jimmy, saying there was no longer anything standing in the way of their happiness.

Maybe she should have phoned, instead. She'd certainly thought about it, but had chickened out. April often got tongue-tied in emotional situations. In a letter, she could collect her thoughts, polish it until she was satisfied she'd selected exactly the right words to express what she meant.

When she didn't hear back from him, she'd assumed he had a new girlfriend and wasn't interested in her anymore. Or that his parents were screening his mail. She wouldn't have blamed the Frosts for wanting to protect their son, after what happened. Her own folks had handled the relationship between her and Jimmy so poorly.

In forbidding April to see him, they'd fed her romantic teen notions. When Jimmy had suggested they purchase ID that upped their ages to eighteen and elope to Vegas, April cast aside her renowned hesitancy and law-abiding ways, and jumped at the chance to be his wife. She'd picked up road maps, planned their route, and outfitted Jimmy's second-hand Honda Civic with camping equipment and food supplies.

Little did she know her parents would devise a desperate finale to crush her dreams.

"Have they been gone long?"

"It happened shortly after we moved away." To another state. The annulment hadn't been enough for her parents. They'd wanted to put as much distance between her and Jimmy as possible.

"They'd been out in the car running errands...and were struck by a man driving home after a night at the bar. My parents were killed instantly. The worst of it was..."

April silently scolded herself for getting teary. Strange how memories were just below the surface. Give them a scratch and a rash of emotion followed. "We'd been arguing before they went out. I'd said things to them that I...I can never take back. The day I finally chose to stand up to them, was the last day they had."

Jimmy's hazel eyes filled with sympathy and understanding. "I'm sure they knew how much you loved them. You were a good daughter. The best." He placed a hand over hers. "What happened to the other driver?"

"God takes care of drunks and fools, they say. The guy walked away without a scratch."

"I hope he served jail time."

"He did. At least I knew he was off the road for a while and couldn't hurt anyone else. That was a comfort."

As Jimmy's touch was now. But the comfort would be fleeting, leaving with him when he drove off in his swanky car.

She slipped her hand out from his. She was a mother now. She had to be strong. She took a moment to watch her son stack snowballs, his super tower way sturdier than her resolve. Or the house.

"This farm was part of my inheritance," she continued. "I rented it for a while but, when the last tenants moved, it sat vacant for more than a year. I tried to sell it and didn't get any takers. My only option was to unload my apartment in the city and move here." She took in the rundown, panoramic view of the farm and let out a sigh. So much work to be done.

Though, now that she'd vented, it didn't feel so overwhelming. She'd always been able to talk to Jimmy, had felt the most true to herself when she was with him. "Thanks for listening."

"Anytime."

He enveloped her in a hug, a friendly one. Two old pals who'd been through a lot together, and even more since.

But, with his body pressed against hers, the camaraderie of the moment faded, replaced with a wave of longing. The atmosphere around them shimmered with heat. She felt jittery and nervous, like a thousand mini trampoline artists were bounding around in her stomach.

He was close enough for her to catch a whiff of his minty toothpaste. Close enough to kiss her.

"*Anytime*...as long as it's this week," she said, stepping out of his embrace. She wasn't prepared to risk her heart to him again, especially when he'd be gone before next Sunday.

Jimmy got the message and backed off, giving her space. "R-r-right. But while I'm here, if you need a hand with anything, just call."

He presented her with a business card, a photo of him looking handsome and rugged, right beside his name and profession—*James Frost, Contractor*. Then he walked away, his footsteps crunching in the snow.

So Marcus was adopted.

That meant April hadn't run off with the first guy she'd seen after their breakup. James' ego had inflated with the news, only to collapse again when April skittered away from him. *Twice*. While he'd

31

almost made a fool of himself and kissed her. In front of her kid, no less.

Though he doubted Marcus would have noticed.

James couldn't afford another slip-up like that. April was right to steer clear of him. Though he'd worked to improve himself since high school, he'd never be a college grad—the kind of man worthy of April's attention. Plus, his lifestyle was nomadic at best, dictated to him by the Getalot expansion.

He went back to his car, started it and drove off, keeping his sights on the road ahead. The most he could hope for with April was to be her friend. Only he was feeling a whole bunch of stuff that went beyond friendship. When he was around her, his chest got tighter, breathing was harder, and all he could think about was touching her, kissing her.

But she'd made it plain she didn't want that. Didn't want *him*.

Probably a good call on her part. James could well imagine an autistic child would put a lot of stress on a relationship. And he'd already seen April in action as a doting mother. Any man who hooked up with her would have to be extremely secure to settle for second place in her heart. And James was through being last on the list.

He was so busy mulling it over, he lost track of how far he'd driven. The covered bridge loomed ahead and, off to one side of it, an old junker rested on the shoulder of the road. A long-legged woman stepped out from behind the wheel, looking desperate.

James pulled his vehicle in front of hers and got out, ready to help her with her problem—dead battery, flat tire, whatever. As he approached, she turned to face him. It was only then that he recognized her. From the cafe.

"Hi, Heather. Did the engine die on you?"

She shook her head. "The car is fine. I followed you out here because...I need to tell you something. In private."

James tensed. He barely knew the woman. Why did she want to talk to him?

"So tell me."

Her eyes glistened. She pulled a tissue from her pocket and swiped at the tears. "This is really hard for me, James. I haven't had the best of luck with men. But that night we met in the bar, I felt like we made a connection. That I could trust you."

Heather tore at her tissue. Bits of it caught on a breeze and floated around them like snowflakes. "You heard about the abandoned baby? That they're looking for the mother?"

James' chin almost hit the pavement. He'd been in town for a day and it looked as if he was about to unravel the mystery that had confounded the locals for a week.

"Do you know who the mother is?"

"Yes." More eye dabbing. "Me."

She teetered, as if about to collapse. He caught her arm, opened her car door and sat her down in the driver's seat. James found a box of tissues in the back and handed it to her. He leaned against the roof of the car and kept his mouth shut, offering silent comfort until she was ready to speak.

"I didn't have enough money for a doctor. I stayed with a friend in Montpelier for several months...to keep my pregnancy a secret here. After Holly came, I panicked. I've just gotten out of a bad relationship and I'm not in a good position to care for an infant. So I put her in the manger at your parents' barn, because I knew your family would look after her. And...it was right that my little girl should be with her grandparents."

He must have heard her wrong. He crouched at her side to get closer. "Grandparents? What are you saying?"

"Sorry. I'm babbling. That's because I never expected to have this conversation with you. I didn't plan to involve you in any of this. But now, I'm at the end of my rope—*past it*—and I can't hold on any longer."

Heather looked at the shredded tissues in her hands and then back up at him.

"You're the baby's father."

Chapter Four

James sat in his car, his fingers numb from strangling the steering wheel, his nerves jangled, as if someone had zapped him with a Taser.

He was a father? How could that be?

He knew all about the birds and the bees, of course. Still, he doubted Heather's story. He'd had one too many drinks that night, sure. They both had. But he couldn't imagine being sober enough to make love to a woman, while too drunk to remember it. Plus, he'd ended up on her couch because he'd made the lucid decision to keep his car keys in his pants.

Not the only thing that should have stayed in his jeans, it seemed.

He drove around aimlessly for hours, his car windows rolled all the way down, hoping for an arctic blast that would help him think straight. He ran his calculations again and again, counting the months backward and forward. No matter which way he did it, it was still nine months since he'd been home for his dad's birthday.

Nine months since he'd slept over at Heather's apartment.

As Frost Farms became visible up ahead, he knew he shouldn't have been driving. He'd been so preoccupied with Heather's revelation he could barely remember the trip. The more he thought about it, the more his head hurt, while the meal he'd had at Kate's soured in his stomach.

He parked his car in front of the house, fired up his cell phone and hit the icon for Amazon. It shouldn't be that difficult to buy a DNA test online. He used the dictation program and spoke the words into the phone, letting it do the typing for him. James sent the purchase to himself care of the UPS Store in Stowe, a fifteen-minute drive away. He'd used their services before, but never for anything so confidential.

Business complete, he slipped into the house, hoping to sneak past everyone until he'd collected his composure. But the whole *fam-damily* was there—his parents, sister Joey, Duncan, Garret, even Lily Parker—and they were all fussing over the baby.

Perhaps *his* baby.

"Hi, Jimmy," his mother said, the infant in her arms. "Would you like to hold her?"

No. Not so much.

It wasn't the kid's fault. Not at all. If there was any blame to be had, it rested squarely upon his shoulders. But he was so torn, his thoughts and feelings so jumbled, he couldn't trust himself to hold Holly. Not while she was staring up at him with those big, innocent eyes.

"She looks pretty comfy where she is," he said, hanging up his jacket.

He had to get proof of his paternity before he did anything stupid. Like get attached to Heather's baby and start thinking of the little girl as his own when she might not be. If he found out Holly was truly his, he'd give her one hundred and fifty percent of his love and support. No question. He was totally ready to accept responsibility for any child he'd helped create.

James stepped past the entrance hall and got a whiff of turnip.

Damn. "Sorry about the vegetables, Mom." He'd completely forgotten his promise to help with them. "I got held up in town and—"

"It's okay, Jimmy." His mother's accepting smile made him feel ten times worse. "Are you all right? You look a little pale."

"Just tired from the drive yesterday," he said, covering. "I'm fine."

"Good," Garret piped in. "Because I want to talk to you about Heather Connolly."

The air around James turned thin, hot. He loosened his collar. "What about her?"

"She was asking for you at Frosty Frolics. I was surprised you knew her."

James wondered how much he should admit to his brother. He decided to stick to the bare facts. "I ran into her at Billy Boy's. Once."

"Well, you must have made an impression. I can't see you with her, though. She's hardly your type."

"I have a type?" Mentally, he reviewed the women he'd been with over the years—all pretty, all petite. James waited for his brother to answer, but the guy looked sheepish, like he'd already said too much.

Their mother stepped forward, speaking in a soft voice. "No matter where you were, Jimmy—crab fishing off Alaska or learning the construction business in Texas—if you sent a photo home, and there happened to be a girl in the shot with you, she looked like April Rochester."

He started to deny it and realized he couldn't. Not without lying. What would Freud say about that?

"Uncle Jimmy! Come see what I got!" Duncan grasped his hand and tugged, dragging James into the living room, and sitting him in the big armchair between the glowing fireplace and the Christmas tree, their homemade childhood ornaments glittering alongside boughs filled with store-bought tinsel and twinkling lights.

Dunc reached down to the floor to grab three children's books and then crawled into James' lap. "Read to me."

James' mouth dried up while his palms went clammy—the same as when he was a boy and asked to read in front of the class. He'd hear the other kids titter as he battled through the words, his voice a halting monotone, his self-worth plummeting.

He'd soon found creative ways to avoid the humiliation. He'd pretend to read from later in the book, making it up as he went. When the teacher told him the correct page number, he'd put on an elaborate show of trying to find the place, drawing it out to waste as much time as he could. When he finally found the right spot, he'd 'accidentally' drop the book on the floor and have to start all over again.

Of course, he could only use that trick once.

Alternately, he'd play sick, or say he had something in his eye. He'd knock over a pile of books, tug on a girl's braid, or start a punching match with the class bully. When he got older, he'd slouch in his seat and sneer like a gangster—a look he practiced in the bathroom mirror. In no time at all, teachers stopped calling on him.

"What have you got here, Dunc?"

Merrily, Duncan listed off the titles. "*How the Grinch Stole Christmas, Rudolf the Red-Nosed Reindeer* and *A Visit from St. Nicholas.*"

James breathed a sigh of relief, as his performance anxiety

diminished. "Let's read that last story, buddy." It was one James knew by heart. He opened the first page and began it from memory.

"'Twas the night before Christmas, when all through the house..."

"Not a creature was stirring," Duncan continued. "Not even a mouse."

"Hey, you did that like a pro." James thumped the kid's shoulder in congratulations. "Maybe you should be reading to me."

The boy took James up on his suggestion, reciting the next two lines perfectly. Then he stalled. Obviously, he'd heard the poem so often he'd memorized some of it, too.

James continued on from there. He called for the reindeer in his best Santa voice, earning a belly laugh from Duncan. Gaining confidence with his recitation, James dropped his volume, half-whispering when he got to the part about listening for the "prancing and pawing of each little hoof" of the reindeer on the roof. He finished with a big flourish, à la the jolly old elf, when he ho-ho-ho*ed* and said, "But I heard him exclaim, ere he drove out of sight...Happy Christmas to all, and to all a good night."

A round of applause startled James and alerted him to the fact they were no longer alone. Lily Parker held the baby, leaving his mother's hands free to clap. Garret gazed at Lily, oblivious to everything and everyone, except the PR manager. And James' father—lean, fit, and looking younger since his retirement—busied himself sorting through the day's mail, glancing up long enough to offer a quick smile. A token show of approval. Sheepishly, James closed the book and handed it back to Duncan.

"Read some more, Uncle Jimmy," he said, cracking open a second story.

"Maybe another night." *And as long as it's a tale I know.*

"Definitely another night," James' father interjected, leading the family into the country-style dining room. "Stories don't get cold but food does. I want to eat mine while it's hot."

Whew! Saved by his dad's appetite.

They took their places at the dining room table, Garret sitting to their father's right, the chosen position for the favored son. James knew he could be oversensitive when it came to the family dynamics and his dad's preferences. That TV psychologist would have a heyday scolding James for trying so hard to impress the parent who was the hardest to please. All he'd ever wanted was for his father to be proud of him. A task he regularly failed. He'd always envied his brother, Garret. Everything came easy for him.

No. Not everything, James reminded himself, as he grabbed his usual seat beside his sister, Joey. Garret had lost a wife and raised his son pretty much single-handedly for the past two years. To get through that took more strength and courage than James could imagine, and he admired his brother greatly.

But they'd never been close. The seven years between them probably had as much to do with it as temperament. Growing up, Garret had his own interests, friends his own age, and James had always felt like he was in the way. Sure, his big brother had been protective, sticking up for him against schoolyard thugs, until James could fend for himself. But he and Garret never hung out much, and when they did, they spent most of the time arguing.

Joey nudged James with her elbow and passed him a serving bowl filled with roasted potatoes. He loaded a couple of spoonfuls on his plate, skipped the turnip and the carrots, took a dollop of horseradish and his share of the beef when the platter came round his way. He poured gravy over the lot.

He shoveled a forkful into his mouth. He had no doubt the meal was up to its usual, delicious standard, but James barely tasted it. The conversation around the large, oval table sounded like a distant buzz. He focused on the portable bassinet positioned in front of the buffet and watched the tiny person sleeping within its pink blankets. James pictured himself picking her up, holding her close, keeping her safe. He envisioned life as a family man—a holiday snapshot of himself, baby Holly and...

Try as he might, he couldn't imagine Heather in that photo. It was April's face he saw, her sparkling eyes and those Cupid's bow lips that begged to be kissed.

Beside him, his father snapped his newspaper and passed it to Garret. The noise and the motion brought James back to reality.

"What's up? Miss the winning Powerball numbers again?"

Garret responded to James' attempt at a joke with a humorless laugh. "Dad's upset about big businesses outsourcing to other countries."

"With all the jobs going overseas," his father chimed in, "where do these hot shots think we're going to get the money to buy their goods? It's economic suicide."

James looked at the two men, confused. "What set this off?"

"The newspaper," Garret said. "Haven't you read it?" His brother didn't wait for an answer. "It's all about this Getalot company and their plans to open a store in Vermont. They buy cheap goods overseas and sell them at discount prices here, while still pulling in a huge profit. It doesn't matter to them that they're putting Americans out of work, or having ten-year-olds in Bangladesh slave fifty hours a week for peanuts in appalling conditions."

James swallowed. That was *his* company they were talking about. He was sure Stephen wouldn't do anything unscrupulous. The man was generous to a fault—a good guy, one of the best, always treating his staff as equals.

James took a swig of water, soothing his dry throat. "What about the jobs Getalot provides in their stores here in America?"

"At minimum wage?"

"With excellent upward mobility and benefits."

Garret sat back in his seat, arms crossed. "How do you know so much about it?"

James figured now wasn't the right time to explain his involvement with Getalot, Inc. And it was never the right time to get into a disagreement with his brother. "I try to stay informed. And it seems to me that a few jobs are what Carol Falls needs."

Garret raised his chin. "We're doing our part to support the local labor force."

"Frost Farms can't employ everyone. What about Verna's husband? Getting him back to work would be a big help to his family."

Their father dropped his cutlery on his plate with a clatter, his exasperation clear, but it was Garret who spoke. "A big conglomerate would be the death of a small town like Carol Falls. Getalot sells maple syrup cheaper than we can by purchasing an inferior product in bulk."

Of course, they did. Not everyone could afford Frost Maple Syrup on a regular basis. That didn't stop poorer families from wanting something sweet and gooey on top of their pancakes. James could well understand how chains like the one he worked for might challenge local companies, but that was the nature of commerce. Wasn't it all about survival of the fittest?

"If businesses can't stay competitive, they shouldn't be in business. Isn't that the American way? By ignoring that, aren't you simply taking care of your own interests. How are you different from the folks at Getalot?"

He'd never seen his brother so red in the face. James half expected the top of Garret's head to pop off. He should have kept his mouth shut.

"Never thought I'd see you side with a big conglomerate over the family farm." Garret stood and motioned to Lily, who gave James an uneasy smile. The two of them left the room with Duncan sandwiched in between, their father in hot pursuit.

"Good going, Jimmy. You must have set a new world's record for clearing the joint."

At last, Joey had said something. Not that it was helpful, but he'd never relied on his little sister to fight his battles. With her athlete's build poured into a police uniform, and their mom's fair skin tones, she looked both tough and fragile. A walking contradiction. She followed on the heels of the others, leaving James and his mother alone.

"I'm sorry, Mom. I didn't mean to get into an argument."

The older woman gave him a squeeze. "You have to remember, Garret's put everything into this farm. It's more than a job to him."

"But what I said...you understand. Don't you?"

"I see both sides. It's the Libra in me. But I won't have my children fighting. I want peace under this roof, Jimmy."

And he was the bad guy, immediately in the wrong because he was a visitor here. James bent his head and examined his socks. "I'll grab my bag and go to a hotel."

He stood to do just that, but his mother clutched his arm.

"That's not what I meant. You're my son and you are always welcome here. But you need to bite your tongue sometimes. Garret, too. And I'm going to say the same thing to him. We're a family...and it's almost Christmas, for goodness sakes. Let's think about the season and be considerate of one another's feelings."

Amazing how she could put things into perspective. She must have seen a rerun of *A Charlie Brown Christmas*.

"Sure, Mom."

He felt bad about fighting with Garret. Not because his beliefs were wrong but because he'd let the conversation with Heather color his mood. And, now that James was alone with his mom, he realized there might be a quick way to solve the paternity of Heather's baby.

"Let me know if you want help with Holly—taking her to the doctor or anything. I assume she'll need a check-up to make sure she's healthy. A blood test might come in handy to help find her parents, too."

"Already done. They're running a DNA profile on her, as well."

He scooped up several plates, preparing to clear the table. "So...did the doctor tell you the baby's blood type? Or is that a police secret?"

"No. He mentioned Holly's O positive. Like most of the folks in Vermont. You included."

Darn. That sure didn't take him off the list of possible fathers. Good thing he'd ordered the DNA kit. There was nothing more he could do now but wait for it.

James took charge of the clean-up and then excused himself, retreating to his room to call Stephen. He got the ego boost he was looking for when he told his employer about the new land alternative he'd discovered that day—April's farm.

"Sounds promising, James. What about public opinion of us there?"

If the discussion at dinner was any indication, it wouldn't be good. "I know these people, sir. I'll mingle with them. Mention it in casual conversation." Not only for Stephen's sake. James wanted to know what folks thought about Getalot for himself.

"Excellent. Call me when you have more, son."

"Will do." James hit the red END button, his pride fortified. Amazing how a short conversation with Stephen could do that. James liked it when the older man called him *son*, too. It fueled his desire to defend the company, more than the paycheck ever could. And the paycheck was enough to win anyone's devotion.

Funny. At one time, he'd felt devotion only for April.

James went to the window, gazing out of it into the darkness beyond and thought about her letter. The one he'd received after she left town.

He'd stood at this very window then too, hurt replaced by hope, as he unfolded the note from its envelope and used the pads of his fingers to trace the neat loops of her handwriting as if it were Braille.

And had as much luck reading it as Ancient Greek.

Embarrassed to ask anyone he knew to tell him the contents, he'd left town, bent on improving himself. Determined to become the man she deserved. The man her parents wanted for a son-in-law.

He'd done whatever he could to make a living, while seeking help for his problem—taking classes, paying tutors. But his efforts came too late.

When he'd returned home to retrieve the letter and finally read it, he discovered the note had been sealed up along with his other treasures—the eagle's feather and the silver dollar.

All lost to him.

James wasn't big on Christmas and had stopped believing in Santa at four when he'd caught his father sneaking presents under the tree, and snacking on the milk and cookies his mother left for the Man in the Red Suit. Getting his Christmas wish was even less likely now that Heather had come back into his life.

In spite of all that, James said a silent prayer, wishing he could erase the years and start over with the woman who'd written the letter buried in the floor beneath his feet.

Chapter Five

Early the next morning, Lily Parker was in a panic. She burst into the kitchen where James and his mother lingered at the breakfast table.

"I can't believe it," Lily said, her gray wool coat unbuttoned and flapping behind her, her red hat askew. "I've got ten kids waiting out there in the snow, equipment in hand, and no instructor."

James gestured for the PR manager to sit. "Slow down and rewind."

Too agitated to stay still, Lily paced by the bay window, the gingham curtains swishing in the breeze she created each time she passed.

"I've been experimenting...with new activities for the farm...to generate extra income during the winter months. Today, I'd planned an introductory class in cross-country skiing for kids. Except the instructor I hired for the morning just called to tell me his wife went into early labor." Lily's voice crept up to a glass-breaking pitch. "He can't be here."

She held her cell phone in one hand, as she madly gesticulated with the other. "I have no idea who to call, Sylvia. Do you know anyone who can fill in on such short notice?"

James mopped up the remainder of the egg yolk on his plate with his last bite of toast. "I could teach the class."

"Really?" Lily's blue eyes rounded and then tapered. "Are you qualified?"

Even though she was desperate, she still wanted to do right by the kids. He liked this Lily Parker.

"Yeah, I'm PSIA certified." She nodded, so he gathered she knew the acronym stood for the Professional Ski Instructors of America. "Years ago, I hung out at Taos Ski Valley in New Mexico, bumming around on the slopes. Worked my way up to a trainer. I mostly taught Alpine but I can do Nordic."

"Oh, Jimmy—I mean, James—if you could step in, I'd be so grateful. I'll give you double what I was paying the other guy. Triple."

He collected his cup and plate and slipped them into the dishwasher. "No need. I'm happy to help out."

She wrapped her arms around James' neck and planted a kiss on his cheek. Yes, he liked this Lily Parker. A lot.

"Don't let Garret catch you doing that, Lily," his mother warned as she cuddled baby Holly, who'd taken up permanent residence on her lap. "Poor Jimmy will have to run for cover."

Once outside, Lily introduced James to his students—children between the ages of seven and twelve. He spent a fun morning showing the kids how to shift their weight by pretending to be Abominable Snowmen, taught them how to use their core when digging in their poles, demonstrated how to stop and, most importantly, how to get up when they fell. They even did some actual skiing. Ninety minutes later, the class ended with happy children, happy parents and a very happy PR manager.

The atmosphere inside his parents' house was a different matter. James' dad spoke to him only in grunts and Garret avoided him completely. So, after a quick shower, James packed his bag. Might as well shove off and inspect Stephen's proposed locations along I-89. A bit of Christmas shopping along the way wouldn't hurt, either. With his belongings safely in the trunk of his car, James kissed his mom goodbye and headed into town to do some snooping.

It was almost lunchtime when he arrived at Kate's Kitchen. Thankfully, Heather's shift was over so he didn't have to talk to her. Nicely ensconced in his captain's chair, James chatted-up the locals over so many rounds of coffee, he thought he'd turn into a fountain. With each person he spoke to, he subtly introduced the subject of big box stores like Getalot and gauged their reactions. The results were mixed, some people saying a nearby outlet would be just what the town needed—more jobs, more shopping. Others were skeptical, with opinions similar to Garret's. A gap as wide as the one between Democrats and Republicans.

Fortified with enough caffeine to keep him wired for a week, James dropped by the police station and asked for his sister, inviting her to lunch at the rustic Hawk & Hound Pub. Stretching to five foot eleven, Joey was almost as tall as James, so when they sat across from each other over their fish and chips, they were practically eye-to-eye.

"I want you to know, I never meant to start a fight during dinner last night."

Joey sighed. "I guess everyone's a little prickly worrying about baby Holly."

Just the opening he needed. "Have you made any progress finding her parents?"

"Actually, it's not my case." She stirred a puddle of ketchup with a French fry and popped it into her mouth. "Kate's younger brother, Erik, caught it."

And contracted the love bug for Joey, if their mother's suspicions were correct. James doubted Erik's feelings were reciprocated, though. No man had captured Joey's interest like James' high school buddy, Noel Fletcher, who left Carol Falls the year Joey turned sweet sixteen.

"So you have nothing to do with Holly's case?"

"No time. I'm investigating the town's mischief problem," she said, absently poking the tight bun she wore to restrain her shoulder-length hair.

"Got any leads?"

"Off the record? It's a strange case. At first, the pranks were laughable, but folks are getting tired of them and the resulting property damage. Slapping up a poster might not seem like much, but when it's on your garage door and it takes you the better part of the morning to scrape it off, you start to get testy. The incidents are escalating, too. I suspect we'll see some real destruction soon. But don't worry. I'll find the culprit. I always do."

"What if you got a tip on the Baby Holly Case? Would you be the one to it follow up? Or would you pass it to Wedge?"

Joey leaned forward, eager. Maybe *too* eager. "Jimmy...do you know something?"

He didn't answer.

"This is serious. The mother may face abandonment charges. More importantly, we want to make sure she gets medical attention. If you know who she is, you need to step forward."

Could he trust Joey to keep his involvement confidential? At least until he could verify his paternity? Or would he be placing his sister in an awkward position, forcing her to choose between her job and family loyalty?

He laughed, hoping she didn't notice how hollow it sounded.

"I've been in town less than forty-eight hours. I haven't had time to play father confessor."

"Why all the questions then?"

Another opening to tell her the truth. James finished his soda before answering. "I'm curious, that's all. Must be my *CSI* addiction."

She pounded her fist on the table and went on a harangue about crime shows raising the lay person's expectations. "People think we can run fingerprints or DNA in five minutes and produce the criminal before the next commercial break. Typical Hollywood."

Joey dotted her lips with a napkin and pushed away from the table, patting her flat stomach. James mopped up as well, and slipped enough cash to cover their bill under his plate, along with a generous tip. He walked Joey back to the cop shop, disappointed that he hadn't learned more from her, namely some inside information that would have let him off the hook in regards to Holly's parentage.

To take his mind off his troubles, he threw himself into his work, scouting alternate land opportunities along the interstate. None were quite as well situated as April's. And she'd mentioned she'd tried to sell her farm. If he could help her with that, wouldn't it be a good thing? Though Stephen Harker had taken James' advice in the past, with favorable results, there was always the possibility the boss would choose a different location. No sense getting April's hopes up about a purchase before James had an offer to make. He ended up at her place, armed with his camera, ready to take photos of the area and email them back to Stephen.

He aimed for some flattering shots of the house. Difficult, because at almost any angle, it was clear the place needed a lot of work, which would lower the market value. Of course, April could always subdivide the land, sell a parcel to Getalot, and keep the home. If so, she'd need someone to fix the roof, at least. And James sure didn't want her getting stiffed by an unscrupulous contractor. If nothing else, he could give her some practical advice on that subject.

He knocked on the door, scanning the yard as he waited. The kid's toys from the day before were gone and Marcus was nowhere to be seen. James banged again and got the same results. Nothing.

As he turned away, he almost tripped over that darned cat, who again hissed at him.

"I missed you, too."

Bandit turned up his feline nose at the sarcasm and trotted off to the nearby barn. Maybe April was there.

James walked over, following a well-tread path through the snow. Nearing the structure, he heard...ocean waves...and then bird calls...with some classical music thrown in between.

The cat, who'd raced him there, sat by the door glaring at him, as if daring him to knock. He did but doubted anyone heard, so he took the liberty of opening the door. Bandit squeezed in between James' legs and ran ahead, to warn his mistress that trouble was on its way, no doubt.

Peering inside, James found April sitting at a potter's wheel, Marcus at her side watching it spin round and round. James closed the door behind him, sealing winter out, and shouted over the canned sound effects of a sudden rainstorm.

April's head jerked up, her mouth forming a surprised O.

"Sorry," he shouted. "I didn't mean to startle you. I did knock."

She flicked a switch on her portable boom box and the storm ended mid thunder crash, plunging the room into silence. A nervous laugh bubbled up from her. "That's okay. I go into my own little world when I'm working with clay."

"That's quite a diverse selection you were playing."

"Sound therapy for Marcus. Autistic kids tend to be sensitive to noise. I'm trying it as an experiment."

What James saw of the interior of the barn didn't look like a science lab. It was fully insulated and downright cozy, a large corner of it set up as a classroom. Not the austere, intimidating ones of his youth. This school looked kid-friendly. Cool.

Small multi-colored chairs surrounded low tables, a variety of games, building blocks and puzzles spilled over every flat surface, inviting play. There was a blue pup tent, an inflatable mattress inside—the perfect kids' nest. A row of whiteboards lined the intersecting walls, drawings and letters sprawled across its face. A giant-sized, three-dimensional mobile of the solar system acted as a canopy to it all, the planets rotating slowly in a beautiful ballet suspended from the barn's high roof.

"This place is incredible."

"Thanks." She stood and stretched, her sweater rising up and exposing a flash of skin that made him miss her next sentence. He pulled it together in time to hear her say, "It's a work in progress, but it's coming along."

With the potter's wheel no longer in motion, her son moseyed over to a half-completed jigsaw puzzle, oblivious to the fact that a third person had joined them. Between the boy's disinterest and the cat's disdain, James' ego took a bruising. He sloughed it off and approached April.

"Is all this for Marcus?"

"For now. Except for my tiny corner here." April gestured with gooey hands to the mound of clay she'd been shaping.

"When did you take up pottery?"

"A few years ago. I thought it might be a good therapy for the children."

"Children?" He swallowed. Did Marcus have siblings? How many? James pictured himself as the Steve Martin character in *Cheaper by the Dozen*, surrounded by a food-splattered brood.

"I want to turn the farm into a center for kids who have learning challenges, much like the Greenwood School in southern Vermont, but for younger children, of both genders. For autistic kids, too. If they don't live nearby, they'll be able to board here. There are certainly enough bedrooms. Of course, I'll need to hire more staff, more teachers. I don't want any child to fall between the cracks."

"Wow. That's quite a project." One perfectly suited to April. It combined two of her greatest strengths—academic smarts and an endless supply of patience. Instantly calmer knowing that a horde of young people weren't set to attack, James appraised the various pots and mugs on the shelves behind April. "These are good. Really good."

Her cheeks pinked, the way they used to when he told her she was the prettiest girl he'd ever seen. "Thanks," she said, again.

"I'm not surprised. You were always skillful with your hands."

When her color deepened, he realized what he'd said could be taken two ways. And, with a sudden rush, he remembered exactly how it felt when she'd threaded her fingers through his hair, and the sweet explorations they'd made of each other as teens while remaining fully clothed.

James unbuttoned his jacket. With the kiln blazing from its cordoned off nook, and the direction his thoughts had taken, the room's temperature jumped several degrees.

"Is there something I can help you with? Or are you just passing by?"

Could he say he was drawn to her like a magnet and not sound cliché? Maybe that he was a kite, tethered to her by a length of twine. How corny would that be? Her nearness made him feel good all over, as if he were high on a cocktail of sugar and sunshine. Plus, he wanted to give her a hand with the plans she had for the house. But Kate had said April was too proud to accept help.

"I got into an argument with Garret," he found himself confessing.

She nodded, as if the subject were old hat. James' disagreements with his brother were legendary. "That's too bad. Did you apologize?"

Hold on. Wasn't she supposed to be on his side? "What makes you think it was my fault?"

Her smile had a been-there-done-that tilt. "You don't have to be in the wrong to make peace."

"True. But we both need some space to cool off before treaty talks can begin. Thought I'd stay in a hotel for a few nights, until things settle down."

"I hope you have reservations, because Christmas is the busy season."

James hadn't thought of that. Damn. "There's always my car, I guess."

"That ride of yours is pretty hot, but not when it dips below freezing, I'll bet."

He took a step closer. "You mentioned your house has spare bedrooms."

April's smile disappeared. Her voice came out with a squeak. "You want to stay here?"

She made it sound like a life sentence. "Just for the week I'm around town. I can pay you room and board."

She turned and busied herself, washing her hands at the nearby sink. "I don't want your money, Jimmy."

Her tone speared him, her words cold and flat, dismissing more than his cash. With one sentence, she'd brushed James off, as well. He almost walked away, and then spotted the throbbing at the base of her neck. He bet her eyes would be green too, but with her looking down, he couldn't tell.

"How 'bout I help out with some chores then," he continued, pleading his case. "I noticed your roof could use a patch job." He pressed himself against the counter, only a breath away from her, yearning to feel that pulse point against his lips. "You're not the only one who's good with their hands."

That blush was back. She dipped her head to conceal it. "That's what I'm worried about."

"I promise to be a gentleman. You'd really be helping me. Garret even more so."

She reached for a towel, mulling over his proposition, he assumed. He gave her the time she needed and held his tongue, picturing what he might do with it to drive her wild. While knowing he had no right to, until he settled things with Heather.

Hands dried, she took a big breath and swiveled to face him. "Okay, Mr. Frost. You can stay in the bedroom off the kitchen. But know this...I plan to work you like a dog."

"Woof."

His comeback earned him a laugh. The best sound he'd heard all day. While the pulse in her neck kept jumping, daring him to kiss it.

And, yes, her eyes were green.

What have I gotten myself into now?

The line ran through April's mind as she led Marcus and Jimmy to the house. She could feel the man's closeness behind her, the heat of him warming her back and making her brain fuzzy. How was she supposed to think straight with him around?

She'd always been a sucker for a hard luck story, and he'd drawn her in with his tale of woe. What a sap she was. All because Jimmy wasn't prepared to eat a little crow.

Still, she could use a handyman. Especially one that came free of charge.

Heading for the snow-covered porch, she saw the place through a stranger's eyes. A year of sitting vacant hadn't helped the exterior of the old home, and there were pressing matters to take care of inside, as well.

She'd been oblivious to it all, too focused on the schoolroom in the barn. *The schoolroom and Marcus.*

She ushered the boys through the front door. They all kicked off their boots and then April helped her son remove his coat, hanging it beside hers. Jimmy took the hint and grabbed an empty hanger for his jacket, which he shrugged out of with a nice rippling motion, muscles flexing beneath the fabric of his shirt.

Lord, help her. The man was fully clothed and had her drooling. How the heck was she going to safeguard her heart while they were under the same roof?

Thank goodness for Marcus. He could play chaperone. If only he'd stop lining up their boots.

Gently, she took the footwear from him and placed it in the hall closet—out of sight, out of mind. Unfortunately, her own obsession wasn't as easy to forget. Especially when he, *Jimmy*, stood mere inches away, giving her a smile that could melt the North Pole. She imagined that mouth on hers, those lips trailing down her neck to her...

"Where would you like me to start?"

She choked and covered it with a cough. "I beg your pardon?"

"With the chores. After I run into town and get supplies, it'll be too dark to patch the roof. Is there something I can do inside tonight?"

April could think of a lot of things. She reminded herself he was talking about the repairs. "You choose. The upstairs toilet leaks and the vinyl tiles in the kitchen have seen better days." Jimmy had always been handy, but she had no idea what he was capable of fixing, so she figured she'd leave the work up to him.

"You got any tools?" he asked.

"Whatever my grandfather owned will be out in the shed. It's locked but I have the key. Hang on to the receipts for anything else you need and I'll reimburse you."

She'd applied for a line of credit to cover the renovation costs it would take to make her dream of a school a reality. Might as well start putting those funds she'd arranged into the buildings now.

"Consider it payback for my lodgings," Jimmy said and added, "I insist," before she could protest. "I'll take a peek at that upstairs bathroom now. Figure out what I need to fix the problem."

"Good idea. Check it out." *While I check out the way you fill those jeans*, she thought, fanning herself as she watched him climb the steps.

James peered around the bathroom. The toilet needed replacing, and the lone window required weather-stripping and new caulking at the very least. Worse, from the condition of the ceiling, it was obvious the roof was leaking. He'd certainly stayed in sorrier places but he hated to see April living this way.

Especially with a child. And during the Christmas season.

His mother had the Frost homestead done up with lights, ornaments, the works. April had nothing—not even a tree in the living room—and, considering how much time she devoted to her boy, probably hadn't given a thought to her surroundings.

At least that was something he could do—make things more habitable for her and Marcus, while helping with renovations for the school she'd planned. And, if he could sell Stephen on the location, April would soon be right next door to a Getalot outlet. She wouldn't even need to cross the street to buy groceries.

Packing all that work into one week would keep James hopping, but he wasn't about to complain. A busy schedule was just the thing he needed to steer his thoughts away from kissing the lady of the house.

Over dinner, April marveled at what Jimmy had accomplished. He'd used her van to swing by Clark's Hardware and purchased a new toilet, which he'd already installed. For that alone, he deserved more than meatballs and cherry tomatoes.

"I'm sorry," she said, apologizing to him again. "I tend to buy only round foods, because that's all Marcus will eat. Peas, blueberries, apricots—"

"How 'bout Brussels sprouts?"

"They might as well be square because, like most kids, he won't touch them."

"We have that in common then. Don't we, Marcus?"

He looked at her son expectantly, as if this one similarity might be enough to form an alliance. The disappointment on Jimmy's face tugged at her heart. He was trying so hard to reach out to Marcus, to include him in the conversation, but her boy was too busy lining up the food on his plate to notice the guest at their kitchen table.

"Is that usual for autistic kids? To eat only round things?"

"Nothing's really usual when it comes to autism, although the children can share similar traits. There's also another challenge that limits Marcus' food choices. I'm weaning him off gluten and casein."

"Casein?"

"It's a protein found in dairy products, along with other food items."

Jimmy's brows weaved together. "What's the deal with gluten and casein?"

Did he really want to know or was he being polite? She didn't want to bore him.

"Autistic children tend to have related stomach ailments. And for some, gluten acts almost like a narcotic." She rose from her chair and walked to the kitchen counter to retrieve a couple of pamphlets on the subject, ones she'd kept to use as examples in creating her own literature about the new school. She held them out to him. "If you're interested, these provide some of the basic facts about the disorder."

He sat back in his seat, eying the glossy brochures as though they might bite. She should have gone with her gut instinct.

He *was* being polite.

Still, he took them from her. April hoped he'd read them, too. She needed someone she could talk to, a friend with a sympathetic ear. She missed having a support system, another adult to help her celebrate the victories and commiserate with her when those triumphs were few and far between.

Could Jimmy be that person? If only for a week?

April craved the closeness they used to share. Seeing him again made her realize that a part of her heart was missing. Hollowed out and empty. Jimmy had filled that void, that loneliness and made her feel whole—loved and wanted in a way no one else ever had.

But that was a long time ago.

There may not be a future for them as a couple now but, sadly, if Jimmy didn't understand what she was going through and the challenges of her son's daily life, there wouldn't be much of a present for them as friends, either.

Alone in the small bedroom off the kitchen, James sank down on the single bed, still holding the pamphlets. He flipped through the top one, his old inadequacies surfacing as he viewed the dense print.

He focused. April wanted him to learn more about her child, and James wasn't going to let her down. He soldiered through the first brochure. It took a while and he was bleary-eyed by the end, but he finished it. He planned to read the other pamphlet the following night.

James reached for his cell phone and, after checking his emails

using a text-to-voice app, he pressed the icon for his old friend—
YouTube.

"Autism," he said into the device's microphone, and spent the
next hour teaching himself more about Marcus, until both he and his
cell ran out of juice.

As he stripped and got under the covers, he formulated a way to
help April and her boy. A scheme James intended to put into action
come morning.

Chapter Six

The next day turned cold, clouds blocking the sun's warmth and leaving the world a dull gray.

Armed with a heavier coat, James spent the morning brushing the snow from April's roof and patching up the spot where the shingles were missing. After lunch, he checked for damage to the attic and that bathroom ceiling. Thankfully, it wasn't too bad. No signs of mold. He planned to take the ceiling down before it collapsed—a big, dirty job he'd start tomorrow. His trip to view commercial properties on the outskirts of Burlington would have to wait until later in the week.

Next on today's list was tackling the sagging porch. Best to hold off until spring to build a new one. He could always come back to town and pay April a visit after the snow thawed. For now, he'd find a way to support the lopsided structure.

His cell phone rang and he glanced at the caller ID before answering. "Hi, Mom. What's up?"

"Just what I wanted to ask you, Jimmy. Mr. Clark told me you were in his store buying building supplies."

Instead of traveling up and down the interstate as he'd intended. Could he blame a doppelganger and get away with it? "April needs some work done on her grandfather's old house."

"April Rochester?" He could hear the smile in his mother's voice. "I think it's wonderful you're giving her a hand. Especially after...well...I'm proud of you. And I have a little something I'd like you to do for me. If you don't mind."

Since he'd missed helping her with the vegetables, he was eager for a chance to redeem himself. "Sure. No problem."

"It's for the Winter Recital I'm co-organizing. Drop by the school at seven p.m. tomorrow. I'll tell you all about it then."

Correction. *Big* problem. He'd tried to avoid driving past his old alma mater on his arrival into town. Now, it looked like he'd have to go inside.

James swallowed his reservations, figuring she needed him to string Christmas lights, a task he could easily get done and get out. "I'll see you there, Mom."

Because he'd always had difficulty keeping appointments straight in his mind, he immediately set his cell to sound an alarm for an hour before he needed to be at the school. No matter what he'd be doing at the time, those sixty minutes would give him enough leeway to wash up, change, drive from wherever he was and arrive when his mother had asked. Thank goodness for smart phones.

After that, he recorded a list of the extra materials he required for April's house. But first, he needed to pick up a very different kind of order. Part of his big surprise.

April spent the afternoon in the barn with Marcus. She used brightly colored letters on a magnetic board to spell simple words.

"Hat." She sounded out the letters as she pointed to them. She then pulled out a baseball cap for each of them to wear and repeated the word.

Bat was next. April switched the H for a B and reached for the plastic, flying creature she'd picked up this past Halloween. She dangled it in front of Marcus and claimed a smile.

And smiles were golden.

"Terrific." She substituted the B for a C, Bandit stepping in for her physical example. "Cat," she said slowly, wondering if Marcus understood that the words represented the items.

Every child was different. Certain treatments and techniques worked better with some kids than others. At this point, she'd be willing to try just about anything. Having been in the system for so long, shuffled between foster parents, Marcus had experienced little consistency in his short life. April vowed to make a difference.

When she'd started teaching, she realized how few resources there were for autistic children, and how little funding. There were no clear paths to take. Every article she read contradicted something else she'd studied. All she could do was give each program a chance and see if it helped. If it did, she plowed ahead with it. If it didn't, she put it to the back of her mind and switched to something else.

It was exhausting, disheartening, but when Marcus took a step forward, she was euphoric.

She had great sympathy for other parents, considering the way diagnoses of autism were on the rise, particularly for boys. It was almost a national epidemic. People were taking out second mortgages to help their children, hoping that early intervention would give their kids a better future. Currently, April was trying biochemical treatments for Marcus, along with diet modification and one-on-one therapy—employing pretty much the same learning techniques she planned to use in her school.

As she packed away her props, she wondered what Jimmy thought of her idea for the farm. He'd seemed enthusiastic. She'd once told him her deepest secrets, her disappointments, her fears, her longings. It would be great to know she could still share those things with him. Even though he was passing through town.

Again, she remembered the letter she'd sent him. Had the post office lost it? Or had Jimmy trashed the note without reading it? Had his parents?

April wouldn't put such an act past her own folks. As much as she'd loved them, they weren't above confiscating her mail. They would have done so to protect her, of course, but they would have destroyed any letters from Jimmy all the same.

The more April thought about it, she couldn't imagine the Frosts doing that to their son. When the four adults had tracked them down in Vegas, she knew his parents were concerned about their teen marriage, but had the feeling they would have supported Jimmy, no matter what. Unlike her own family, who'd threatened her new husband, demanded a speedy annulment and whisked April away to live in another state—leaving no forwarding address.

Now that Jimmy was staying with her, she could resolve the old mystery and find out what happened to her letter.

She glanced at her watch. Instead of moving on to another round of lessons, April decided to pack it in, hoping she could get more into her son's stomach than an apple and a couple of chicken balls at dinner. She solicited Marcus' help putting away the remainder of their learning aids, and then bundled him up in his boots and jacket, Bandit following at their heels.

The sun had set just past four, so April turned on the outside flood lights she'd had installed to guide them on the snowy path. Approaching the front door of her house, she saw a miracle and clapped her hands together, ready to cheer. The porch didn't slant anymore. Jimmy had propped up the old wooden boards with cement blocks. *Genius.*

Her own mood lifted, too. Until she entered the house and a mechanical whine from some sort of power tool had Marcus flattening his hands over his ears. She couldn't persuade him to lower his arms long enough to remove his coat and gave up trying.

Steering him along in front of her, April followed the sound and froze at the archway to the kitchen, her heart grabbing.

Jimmy was on his knees, a corded scraping gizmo in his hand. He'd stripped most of the old kitchen tiles. He'd also stripped himself, to the waist, his upper body gleaming with perspiration. The picture he made had her sucking in a breath, her flesh warming in spite of the cold trek from the barn to the house. She'd thought him a hunk in high school. Now, he had a man's body—muscled and naturally so. Not like he pumped iron in a gym but that he'd done physical labor.

He looked up and caught her staring. Maybe he'd sensed her there or maybe he'd heard the appreciative moan that escaped her mouth.

Jimmy turned off the machine, leapt up and threw on a T-shirt, spoiling her view. "I'm sorry. I didn't expect you back so soon, or I wouldn't have used the electric scraper." He crouched in front of Marcus. "And you know, buddy, some women think we boys have a lot in common with power tools...because we tend to make a bunch of racket but it's hard to get us to work."

Marcus didn't react to the joke, but he did lower his hands as soon as the noise stopped, and was now struggling out of his jacket, the sound forgotten. Again, April felt sorry for her new boarder. Jimmy was trying so hard to bond with Marcus and striking out at every turn.

"Humor is difficult for autistic kids, Jimmy. Their take on the world is very literal. Don't let it bother you."

She could tell it did, though, no matter how much he tried to mask the blow. A few seconds later, his expression morphed into curiosity. "What's he doing now?"

April glanced around and found Marcus by the pile of old, torn up tiles. He pulled out several pieces and examined their shapes. With astonishing ease, he located exactly where they'd originally sat and placed them there again, as if the floor were a giant-sized jigsaw puzzle and he was putting it back together.

An outstanding skill but completely counterproductive to Jimmy's work.

"Autistic children tend to be good spatially," she explained, wishing she'd taken more time to think through these renovations. Could Marcus handle the changes? The new vinyl tiles were as close to the original color and pattern as Jimmy could find at the local hardwood store. She hoped that attention to sameness would reduce Marcus' anxiety level, once the new floor was installed.

How well would Jimmy cope with her son's behavior, in the meantime?

"It's really cool he can do that." Her handyman looked genuinely impressed. April smiled. She thought it was pretty cool, too.

"What you've accomplished in a single day is also amazing."

"The best is yet to come," Jimmy promised, rising. "Ready for supper?"

The kitchen table stood in the corner, its four chairs piled on top. It was a small task to set it all to order, and she headed over to do just that.

"Don't worry about the table. I have something else in mind." He strolled to the fridge, opened it and pulled out several plastic bags. "A picnic."

Overwhelmed by his thoughtfulness, she almost leapt into his arms. "When did you have time to make a picnic?"

"I didn't. I asked Kate to put something together for us...all gluten and casein free. With lots of *round* foods. She used a melon baller on some cantaloupe and to shape a cheese substitute that tastes surprisingly good. I hope Marcus likes it."

Had the guy read a book on how to win the heart of a single mother? "That so sweet, Jimmy. Thank you."

He smiled and dipped his head, as if embarrassed. "Shall we find a nice spot to eat...under a tree, perhaps?" He gestured toward the living room.

The way Jimmy's eyes sparkled, she knew he had something out of the ordinary in mind. He'd always been daring and impulsive, qualities that evened out her tendency to hesitate and overanalyze. The yin to her yang.

But she really hoped he didn't intend on eating their picnic outside in the snow.

April took Marcus by the hand and drew him across the hall. The coffee table was moved in tight to the couch and a large blanket lay on the floor in its place. Jimmy had positioned toys nearby for Marcus. Plates and napkins were set and ready for use.

His efforts made her heart swell. She kissed Jimmy on the cheek, the soft scratch of stubble tickling her lips.

As she turned her head, she saw the other surprise she hadn't noticed at first. Now she understood his reference to a tree wasn't merely an allusion. In the corner of the room was a newly chopped pine, mounted and sitting in a bucket, waiting to be decorated.

Marcus noticed the tree at the same time. And started screaming.

James had heard kids holler before—because they were hurt, scared or plain wilful. Marcus sounded like someone was skinning him alive. Bandit cowered and ran for cover, diving under the couch.

"What's wrong with Marcus?"

April flinched at every high-pitched squeal. She assessed the boy with concern but kept her cool. "I think it's the tree. He doesn't handle change well and having it there, where he usually keeps his toys—it's messing with his need for order and familiarity. That, along with the new kitchen tiles..." She pursed her lips. "I'm sorry, Jimmy. The tree was really thoughtful of you, but I think we'd better put it out on the porch."

She moved to help him, but he waved her away. "I can manage." He needed a moment to collect himself, to recover from...

James wasn't sure what. The disappointment, he guessed. He'd tried to help, to do something nice, expecting to make April and Marcus happy. Instead, he felt like he'd gone twelve rounds with a professional boxer—beat up and thrown out of the ring.

While April held the door open, James carried the tree out of the house, careful not to slop water from the bucket on the floor. Outside in the cold, he positioned the pine in the far corner of the porch, away from the windows and out of sight, and contemplated his own disappearing act. His first thought was to get in his car and press the pedal to the metal, because if Marcus reacted this way to the Christmas tree surprise, how would the picnic go over?

James listened at April's front door. All quiet on the western front. He gathered up the tattered remnants of his chutzpah and entered the house, the warm air heating his chilled arms.

April sat on the blanket, Marcus playing quietly at her side, absorbed with his building blocks. "Sorry about that," she said, with a shy smile. "Tantrums go with the territory."

"I thought maybe he was an environmentalist, protesting the fact I cut down a tree."

She laughed. "No, not an environmentalist. Well, not especially." April cocked her head to one side to look at her son. "He can't verbalize his displeasure, so screaming tends to be his go-to reaction. I'm really sorry, Jimmy. Please, don't take it personally."

Typical of April to apologize though it wasn't her fault.

"I should have asked you before bringing a Christmas tree into your house," he said. "I mean, you could have converted to Judaism for all I know."

"*Oy vey.*"

Her comeback cut the tension. His shoulders relaxed.

"Seriously, Jimmy...if you'd talked to me about it ahead of time, I would have said, 'Great idea. Go for it.' I wouldn't have anticipated his meltdown, either. Trees don't normally bother Marcus. He can walk around a park as well as any ten-year-old boy. *Honest.* I guess he just didn't expect—"

"A pine in his living room."

"Exactly. So..." She waggled her eyebrows. "How about some food? Whatever you've got there smells delicious."

James knelt beside her. "I'm almost afraid to open it."

"You've already seen the worst Marcus can offer. Dinner should be a breeze."

"Famous last words," he muttered as he reached into the first bag. He put all the containers on the blanket and began doling spoonfuls of food on their plates—including a rounded fish cake and a salad that combined rotelle, pearl onions and cherry tomatoes. James hoped the gluten-free pasta looked enough like wagon wheels to gain Marcus' favor.

"Whoa, Jimmy. That's more than enough for me. Your presentation is very good, though."

"I've worked in a restaurant a time or two."

"Sounds to me like you've done everything."

I've never made a kid scream before, he thought but didn't announce.

April took a bite of the pasta salad and then leaned back with a contended sigh. "This is wonderful." Her satisfied grin carried a ray of sunshine with it. "Thank you, Jimmy Frost. You are the best."

It was on the tip of his tongue to correct her and say *James*, but his tongue had other ideas. It wanted to lick that daub of creamy dressing from the corner of her mouth, and then kiss her until she was senseless.

He reached for his napkin, instead, and dabbed her lips, his knuckles brushing her cheek. That slight touch heated his blood, filled him with want and need. He let his fingers trace the curve of her neck. The place he used to trace kisses.

"Jimmy, don't."

"Don't what?"

She swept the hair from his eyes, and then her hand dropped back to her side. "Don't tempt me."

Unfair, because she was so darned tempting. He wouldn't have believed he could ache for someone, but he did—wanted to hold her so bad his chest hurt. But he had no right to her. Not while he was caught in a tangled mess with Heather and her baby. A child he might have made during a drunken one-night stand.

Knowing he'd behaved so irresponsibly disgusted him. The fact that April's parents were killed by a drunk driver, only added to his burden. He couldn't involve her in any of his troubles. He backed away just as Marcus carried his full plate into the kitchen.

"We never eat in the living room," April said, apologetically. "I don't think he understands it's allowed."

They followed Marcus. He'd already positioned his chair in its usual spot and was, once again, trying to piece the old tiles together. The job held his attention for a while but, finally overwhelmed by the enormity of the task, he sat in the middle of the room and screamed and kicked and cried.

James felt...*awful*. He'd done this to Marcus, upset the kid with the renovations, the tree and the picnic.

"It's been an exciting day," April said, drawing her son close and giving him a bear hug. "I think he needs some quiet time to decompress. Could you give us a few minutes alone, please?"

James watched, puzzled. "I'm not criticizing, but if you hug him when he has a tantrum, aren't you encouraging—"

The look April shot him said—*Zip it, if you want to keep your vital organs.* "Read the pamphlets I gave you. Then we'll talk."

James gave himself a mental note—never question Momma Bear

about her parenting skills.

While Marcus fought and hollered, James cleared their picnic and folded the blanket. He placed the food back in the fridge and raced to the small bedroom he'd claimed as his own, planning to do the dishes later.

He picked up the second brochure, devoured its words and, when the house was quiet, and both April and Marcus were in bed, James spent another night with YouTube. After observing one particular video of an autistic child having a meltdown, he understood how April had tried to help her son. And James came up with a little strategy of his own.

Chapter Seven

April woke, squinting at the morning sun, her head full of cotton. Sleep deprivation was the name of the game when it came to parenting Marcus. How he functioned on so little rest was a mystery to her. Whenever he slept, she did too, with one eye open and an ear cocked to his room. With his inability to recognize danger, a shard of glass might seem like a fun toy, while a plush bunny could invoke cries of fear.

Truth be told, something else had caused her restless night—Jimmy's crack about hugging Marcus. It proved he hadn't read the pamphlets. Yes, she knew he'd been busy. She got that. And appreciated all the work he'd done for her. But how long did it take to read a brochure? Ten minutes? Moral support went a long way, and he'd seemed interested in learning more about autism, about cheering on her efforts. Had that only been lip service?

She threw on a coral top and a pair of brown jeans, while Bandit did figure eights around her ankles. The cat followed her down the hall where they both listened at her son's door, hearing the noises he made. Not language but sounds, at least. When she'd first met him in her classroom, he was either silent or screaming. Nothing in between.

April entered Marcus' room, and he made eye contact, filling her heart with so much love she thought it might burst. He kicked off his covers, his feet on top of the blankets. She lifted one foot, pressed her lips against the instep and blew. The giggles she got in return were worth the extra hours of sleep she'd missed. She lived for these moments.

"Shall we go downstairs, my darling? Get some breakfast?"

She selected an outfit for him. Expecting him to decide what to wear on his own would take hours. Too many choices overwhelmed him.

April could relate. She'd experienced her own brand of existential angst regarding fashion before she'd simplified her wardrobe for the move back to Carol Falls. She currently had three rules for each garment in her closet—it had to fit, it had to match with at least four other pieces she owned and it had to wash up nicely. No ironing involved.

As she led Marcus down the stairs, the aroma of coffee wafted past her nose, a spicy Christmas blend she'd purchased especially for the season. At the bottom step, she headed for the kitchen but Marcus pulled the other way, stopping to gawk out the living room window. A shock in itself. He never bothered much with windows, or whatever was on the other side of them.

Curious, she walked over and saw the thing that drew his attention—the Christmas tree. The pine was still on the porch outside but now its branches shimmered with decorations—gold and red balls, tin stars, a humungous heart ornament and, from the very top, a beautiful angel smiled down at them. Marcus pointed at the tree, his eyes wide. Amazingly, Jimmy had turned something that disturbed her son into an object that inspired awe.

She and Marcus ran to the kitchen to find the man behind it all and discovered another surprise. The floor was finished, the new vinyl tiles installed and the table set for the first meal of the day. Jimmy must have worked into the wee hours of the night, or rose early that morning to complete the job.

This was better than Christmas.

A flood of excitement spread through her tired limbs. Her fingers trembled with anticipation. With the improvement, she visualized others. She could knock down the wall separating the kitchen and dining room and put in a larger table to accommodate more children. And paint! She imagined the cabinets a perky lemon-lime, the doors and the trim a fern green, and accents of orchid and sweet pea to make it all pop. The boarding school took shape in her mind in a way it never had before. Thanks to Jimmy.

She forgave him on the spot.

The man was a godsend. Not to mention, easy on the eyes. If she wasn't careful, she'd end up falling in love with him all over again. Considering his presence already put her off balance, falling would be an easy next step.

Marcus inspected the new tiles, traipsing over every row. Apparently satisfied, he plunked himself down at the table. She gave him his usual orange and a few choice leftovers from the picnic, before knocking on Jimmy's door. But there was no answer. She poured a cup of coffee, locking the scent into her lungs. And that first sip? Pure ambrosia. April consumed half the mug before registering the sound of running water—Jimmy showering in the downstairs bathroom.

That made her salivate more so than the coffee.

She'd never seen him naked. Bare-chested, yes. He often went shirtless that summer when he'd helped out on her grandfather's maple syrup farm. The work arrangement effectively separated Jimmy and his brother and, since April's grandfather sold most of his raw product to the Frosts, it served to keep the business in the family.

Chores done, she and Jimmy would find a secluded spot to kiss and cuddle, April skimming her hands over Jimmy's tanned skin. A few times, they'd gone off on their bikes, cycling the distance to the nearby waterfall, the source for the town's name and the river that ran through it. They'd dance in the fall's spray, kissing the droplets off each other's cheeks.

He'd never pressured her to do more.

She knew some boys who'd tell a girl anything to score a homerun. One of her classmates, Tiffany Morse, gave in, sacrificing her virginity, her reputation and her diploma. Poor Tiff dropped out of school at fifteen when she could no longer hide her baby bump under bulky sweaters.

As far as April knew, the father of the child never accepted responsibility. So unlike Jimmy. He'd always been a gentleman and wanted to get married before starting a family. He'd loved and respected her, and that's why he'd been willing to wait.

She knew it hadn't been easy for him. Naive as she'd been in the ways of lovemaking, it would have been impossible to ignore the physical proof of how much he'd wanted her. The fact he'd denied himself made her feel both desired and cherished. Their hands may have wandered, but their bodies remained clothed.

At least below the waist.

Now, she fantasized about what he'd look like coming out of the shower, the water dripping from his hair, his skin wet. She might have been a good girl in high school, but now that she was a woman—a woman with a very attractive boarder—it didn't hurt to daydream a little.

Lost in her thoughts, she didn't hear the shower shut off, didn't hear the bathroom door open. The next thing she knew, Jimmy stood in the hallway, still damp from the water's spray and holding a tiny towel around his waist.

"Sorry. I didn't know you were awake."

Dear Lord, help her. The guy should have been Scottish, the way he could fill out his makeshift kilt. Were men supposed to have such shapely legs—muscular and toned? Could she be arrested for ogling? Distracted by his closeness and the sudden rush of awareness that engulfed her, she spilled coffee all over her new kitchen floor.

"Let me help you wipe that up."

Was there any chance he'd use that teensy towel?

Bad idea. April forced herself to focus. "You'd better get dressed." *Quickly. Please. Before I jump you.* "I'll have this cleaned in a jiff." Bandit was already doing his part, lapping it up.

Jimmy grinned and disappeared behind his bedroom door.

She grabbed a wad of paper towel. First, she wiped away the sweat that had popped up between her breasts and then mopped the floor, admiring Jimmy's handiwork. He'd done a great job. At the rate he was going, he'd have her whole house renovated in a week, a notion that left her jutting out her bottom lip in a pout.

If she devised extra projects, would it entice him to stick around?

Before she could think of any, she heard an unfamiliar sound—a light tittering, followed by a true guffaw. She turned to find Marcus laughing, *really* laughing, like he'd heard a terrific joke.

"What is it, sweetie? What's so funny?"

She followed his line of vision to the pantry door. When she opened it, she saw exactly what had him in stitches. She'd accidentally put the hot coffee pot on one of the shelves.

April had to laugh, too. A laugh filled with joy. Marcus had found humor in the moment—a huge breakthrough for him. It justified the expensive treatments and all the extra work she'd done with him in the classroom. She couldn't have been more thrilled.

She ran to Jimmy's room, burning to tell him the good news. Hand up, ready to knock, she froze. How could she explain the coffee pot incident without confessing the reason behind it?

That seeing him half-naked made her lose her mind.

James dressed on a high. Although he hadn't meant for April to catch him running around in a towel, he was sure she'd been checking him out. And he'd never been quite so happy for a woman to give him the once-over.

Was she as attracted to him as he was to her?

He loved the way she sighed to herself when she was thinking, loved her gentle nature. Her feistiness, too. She was a champion for her boy, and James admired that kind of passion.

Yet...

He knew Marcus had social issues but, more than anything, it bothered James that the kid ignored him. It made him feel as insignificant as he had during his own childhood. Maybe that's why he'd landed in trouble back then.

Nothing serious. Not compared with some of the antics teens got involved in these days. He was never into drugs. Never stole. Never destroyed property. He'd gotten into a few fist fights, defending himself when other boys called him stupid. Even though he suspected what they'd said was a fair assessment.

More than suspected. He'd hit them because they'd spoken the truth. He *was* stupid. Other kids easily stood up in front of the class and read aloud. James couldn't. He'd start to sweat and his stomach would churn, while the words in front of him swirled.

Would any child he fathered wind up with the same problem? Would Holly?

It was time to find out.

He'd received a call from the UPS Store in Stowe that his parcel had arrived. When he purchased the online DNA kit, he'd watched a video that showed how to do the cheek swabs. He'd need one for himself and one for the baby. And, unless he wanted everyone in his family to know about his indiscretion, he'd have to find some time alone with Holly to obtain the sample.

If he were her father, he would, of course, take responsibility. But he prayed, with all his heart, he wasn't.

There was something about Heather. Something that wasn't quite right. Sharing a baby with her wasn't going to be easy. While having a child with April...

That seemed like a dream come true.

By the time Jimmy made his 'clothed' appearance, April had Marcus bundled up and ready for some outdoor fun.

"Want to join us?" she asked, admiring how Jimmy's long-sleeved tee hugged his shoulders. Fully dressed he was still a danger to her senses. Not only because of his good looks. She loved the way he smelled, even without cologne. Just the hint of bar soap on his skin was enough to make her pulse jump. And his hair, still damp from the shower, was thick, shiny and oh, so touchable.

She stroked Bandit's back instead, his fur warm from sunning himself on the living room's window ledge. "How about you, kitty-cat? Are you coming with us?"

His mewed response sounded very much like a 'No'. He yawned, put his head on his paws and closed his eyes.

Jimmy threw on his winter wear and accompanied her and Marcus outside. As they passed the tree on the porch, Jimmy dragged it a foot closer to the door, catching her son's attention. His expression wavered between interest and wonder.

"What's with the tree, Jimmy? Looks great, by the way. Marcus thinks so, too."

"I figure if I can get him used to it, while inching it closer every day, I can eventually move it back inside the house."

A solid plan. "Good idea."

"Oh, and I get what you were doing yesterday with the tantrum—using a deep compression hug as a comfort, while preventing him from hurting himself."

So he'd read the pamphlets. He understood. "*You* deserve a hug for that. And for all the work you've done." She slipped her arms around his waist.

It started as a simple thanks. It didn't stay that way. Not once he returned her embrace. She'd almost forgotten how perfectly they fit together—her head resting on his chest, her body molding to his.

"Sorry I questioned you," he said, his voice husky. "It wasn't my place."

She wished it was. That they could be partners again. As friends, as parents, as lovers. Did he feel the same? Yearn to rekindle what they'd felt for one another in the old days?

"I wrote to you, Jimmy. After my parents separated us. Didn't you get my letter?"

His body tensed. "I didn't read it, no." He pulled away, holding her at arm's length. "What did you write?"

Did it matter now? If he hadn't received the note that meant he hadn't rejected her. They were starting over with a clean slate.

"It's not important anymore. I'm just glad you're here."

With Marcus holding one of her hands and Jimmy grasping the other, they trundled around to the side of the house to where she stored her son's outside playthings.

"Want to build a fort? Or an igloo?" she asked her boys.

Jimmy dug through the snow and found the buried rope of Marcus' toboggan. "How 'bout a ride? We can use this on that hill out back."

She encouraged Marcus to have a seat on the sled. Jimmy pulled it along behind him, while she walked at his side, hand in hand again. "Marcus hasn't actually made it down the hill. He jumps off every time."

"Why don't you ride with him then?" Jimmy suggested. "I'll wait for you at the bottom."

April agreed and, once they had the sled in position, she sat down behind her son. When Jimmy was in place, he blew on his bare hands and then waved, urging her on. April dug her heels into the snow and inched forward, bit by bit until the sled was at the apex of the slope. With a final push, the toboggan began its downward descent.

The wind whipped her cheeks, and the snow flew over her in a wave, sneaking past her collar and sending tingles down her back. Her laughter echoed through the maple trees, as they whisked by. It felt wonderful to act silly, to be a kid again.

Too soon, the ride slowed and came to a stop. April hopped off the toboggan and scooted around to the front of it so she could gauge her son's reaction.

"Did you like that, Marcus?" The boy responded with a cautious smile. "I think he did."

"Let's try it again then, shall we?"

Together they walked back up the hill, Jimmy pulling Marcus on the sled. Once they reached the top, Jimmy brought the ride to its starting point and gestured to it, bowing slightly, as an old-fashioned courtier might.

"Your ride awaits you, mademoiselle."

"Why don't *you* go this time?"

Jimmy shot a glance at Marcus. "Will that be okay?"

"We'll find out. Besides, I want to take a photo as he's coming down the hill. Give me a moment to explain it to him."

She helped her son off the toboggan and invited Jimmy to sit. "Marcus will need some time to get used to you there. He's got touching issues. Especially with people he doesn't know very well."

"What can I do to help?"

"As little as possible, actually. Just stay quiet and still and give him his space. Hopefully, he'll see everything's okay and choose to join you." April pulled her cell phone from her coat pocket and showed it to her son. "Mommy wants to take a picture of you on the sled with Jimmy. I'll be right at the bottom of the hill waiting for you."

Marcus was a visual kind of kid and used to her taking photos. In fact, on good days, he could be a bit of a ham in front of the camera. She snapped a few shots of Jimmy alone on the toboggan. With any luck, it would motivate her son to join in.

She high-stepped it through the snowdrifts, glancing back several times along the way to check how Marcus was coping. He watched her, his face tight. He circled the sled, looking at it, and Jimmy, and then at her.

At least he wasn't screaming.

April waited at the bottom of the hill. She hit the zoom on her camera app and framed her picture. Now, all she needed was for her subject to cooperate.

He walked around the sled again, and then stared at the leafless trees. April was about to give up when Marcus stepped into the front of the toboggan and sat down. He didn't appear terribly happy, but at least he was onboard.

Jimmy looked uncomfortable, too—his extra height folded on the short sled, his knees up by his shoulders, ready to jump off at any moment should her son protest.

Poor guy. She'd given him an impossible task. How the heck was he supposed to keep his distance from Marcus on a toboggan?

For both their sakes, April didn't dawdle. "Ready," she hollered.

Jimmy shuffled forward until the sled shot over the edge of the rise. Marcus's mouth opened. He didn't seem afraid. Mostly surprised.

April kept her index finger busy snapping shots. It appeared as if they were going faster—maybe from the compacted snow of the previous run, maybe from Jimmy's extra weight.

"Watch out," he called.

April looked over the phone to find them headed straight for her. She was about to leap out of their path when Jimmy leaned to one side, steering away from her, and then he bailed. He rolled once and ended up flat on his back, while Marcus and his toboggan came to a graceful stop at her side.

April couldn't help but laugh at the vision of Jimmy splayed out on the ground.

"I don't know what you think is so funny about a man making an angel," he said, with a grin. He pushed his legs out and swept his arms through the snow.

"Nice cover story." She reached around to grab the toboggan rope and found the ride empty. Marcus stood a few feet away from Jimmy. Watching.

April held her breath. Was her son forming a connection? Noticing Jimmy for the first time?

Neither adult said a word. Jimmy slowed his movements and, with care, stood and stepped away from his creation. They watched together, in awe, as Marcus bent down, touched the outline in the snow and then gazed up at the man who'd made the angel.

Jimmy beamed, looking as happy as April had ever seen him. As happy as when they'd said their wedding vows. At last, Marcus had acknowledged him, had actually made eye contact. Another huge advance.

A second later, her son picked up a twig. And another. He plunked his rear down in the snow and lined up the sticks, ignoring Jimmy and the angel, as if they didn't exist.

Had she imagined the connection? Wanted it so badly she'd heaped more meaning on the moment than actually existed? If so, it was clear Jimmy had been fooled, too. The man looked like someone had slapped him, and a second memory from their wedding day flooded back to April. The arrival of her parents and their threats against him.

She clapped a hand over her mouth, muffling a sob. She was used to the two-steps-forward-one-step-back dance she and Marcus engaged in every day.

Jimmy wasn't.

Her heart broke for him. And for herself. Because, for a minute there, the three of them had felt like...

A family.
Now, they were the furthest thing from it.

Nothing like a little destruction to work out one's frustrations.

Although James didn't relish the dirty job of knocking down the bathroom ceiling, it would help him let off steam. Not that he was angry. More disheartened. He really thought he'd made some headway with Marcus. Sorrier still, he'd lied to April about the letter. Lied by omission.

Time for a little down and dusty with seventy-year-old plaster.

He'd already opened the outside window and laid a heavy sheet of plastic over the bathroom floor and fixtures. As well, he'd created a plastic wall in the adjoining hall to act as a protective barrier for the rest of the house. He wore long sleeves, long pants, gloves and a hat that covered his ears. Donning his respirator and goggles, he figured he looked like an underwater sea diver, minus the oxygen tank and fins.

First, he scored the joint where the ceiling met the walls with a utility knife, making a clean cut. Next, he went at the plaster, ripping away the loose bits and then tackling the rest of the ceiling with a pry bar and sheer determination, until he was down to the wooden laths.

It took him twice as long to clean up as it had to tear down. Fortunately, he'd found an old wheelbarrow in the tool shed, which made hauling out the debris much easier. Apart from a trip to the dump, he was done for the day. At least on his house repairs.

Washed, changed and bundled up, James trudged across April's snow-covered property, snapping photos and taking videos of the place to send to Stephen Harker. Despite its neglect, the sugarbush was in good shape. It was a pity to cut it down for a parking lot, but sacrifices had to be made in the name of progress.

James wandered over to the special tree where he and April had spent most of their time and traced the letters he'd carved into the bark so long ago—J. F. & A. R., with a big heart surrounding them.

Maybe he'd ask if they could leave that one tree standing. He took a photo of it on his cell phone, to be on the safe side. When his device rang, he stole a glimpse at the caller ID.

"Hi, Stephen. I was about to email you some pictures."

"I'll watch for them. Gotta say, James, I'm impressed with the new location you've suggested. Any idea what this woman wants for a price?"

"I'm working on that now, getting appraisals from similar farms in the area."

"Good. How about public opinion? What do the townfolk of Maple Falls think of a having a Getalot store in their area?"

"It's *Carol* Falls, sir. And the feelings are mixed." James switched the phone to his left hand, shoving the right one in his coat pocket to warm it.

"Same old, same old. Get me some figures, son."

Stephen ended the call as James reached the house. With the roof patched and the front porch jury-rigged, the exterior was as presentable as it was going to get for now.

Hopefully, it would be enough to win April a good price, if she chose to sell it along with the land. If not, he'd given her a hand starting the school of her dreams, and that went a long way to lift his spirits.

After his trip to the dump in April's van and a fast jaunt to Stowe to pick up his package, James, still wearing his work clothes, drove to meet his mom. No point showing up in a suit, if his mother wanted him to hang garland. But, as he walked up the steps of White Pine Ridge High, he wished he'd worn something better, to give his ego a boost after what happened with Marcus. Or hadn't happened, as the case turned out to be.

Though James stood well over six feet, seeing the arches of his old school made him feel as small and insignificant as when he'd first entered its halls so many years ago. He forced himself to step into the cavernous entryway, his footfalls echoing on the well-trodden tiles. The place even smelled the same—like paper, wooden pencils and teen sweat.

Or was that him?

He headed for the auditorium, the sound of muted voices growing louder as he approached. Probably a whole decorating committee was on hand.

James stopped as he reached the open door, surprised at the number of people he saw. He'd clearly walked into a rehearsal. Chairs were set up for an audience, a mix of adults and kids scattered in the seats. At least two dozen children were on stage. Those in the first row sat on the floor, the middle row stood, and the back row balanced on a long, low bench for height, so that everyone could be seen.

"Let's take it from the top, please. Big smiles, everyone."

A piano intro played. The kids launched into a rendition of *Jingle Bells*. Some sang out with gusto. A few had that deer-in-headlights expression and half-heartedly joined in the chorus. A couple of children on either end of the first row shook bells, more or less to the beat of the music.

Very cute.

As James scanned the group, he saw his nephew, Duncan. About the same time as Dunc saw him. The boy waved and made a move to dive off the stage and run to James, but an adult supervisor motioned him back in place.

Someone squeezed in behind James and it was only then he realized he was blocking the door. He excused himself and stepped to one side, out of the way. Immediately, he felt a hand on his arm.

"Thanks for coming, Jimmy," his mom whispered.

"What's going on here?"

"It's been a while since the town had a Winter Recital. Mrs. Hoadley approached me and we decided to organize one. There'll be music, recitations, a couple of skits..."

James remembered his Grade Nine teacher and her encouraging hugs. She sat at the piano, plucking away at the keys—a stocky woman with round glasses, soft curls and energy to burn.

"Sounds great."

"I knew you'd like the idea. You always had an artistic flair. That's why..." His mother bit her lip, looking shy and hopeful at the same time. "That's why I'd like you to participate."

Oh, man. It took every ounce of nerve he'd had to step foot in the school. Now she wanted him to perform in it?

"Look, Ma. I'm kinda..." *Busy* was the next word on his tongue. But she gazed up at him with those big eyes of hers, the ones he found hard to refuse. Maybe it would be good for him to contribute. Other than sports, he hadn't really participated at school. This would be a way of overcoming his demons, to put them to rest, once and for all.

"You want me to sing something? Accompany someone on the guitar?"

"No." She placed a book in his hand. "I want you to do a

reading."

His stomach felt like it was on the wrong end of a bungee cord, and plunging fast."

"You did such a terrific job reading to Duncan the other night. Children love *Pete the Cat Saves Christmas*, and it's so similar to *A Visit from St. Nicholas*. Both the kids and their parents will get a huge kick out of it."

James stared at the cover, a cartoon cat in a Santa hat popping out of a chimney.

"Mom, I..."

How could he tell her? How could he admit to her something he hadn't told anyone else? That he denied to himself?

"Please say yes, Jimmy. I want to show you off to the town."

Show him off? More likely, he'd show himself *up* if he stood on the stage and sputtered.

Maybe the story was available as a talking book. He was good at memorization. If he heard it a few times, he'd have the piece down pat.

"Oh...did your friend find you?" his mother asked.

"My *friend?*"

"Garret's seen an old car at the farm a couple of times in the past few days. He thought the driver looked like Heather Connolly."

Damn. He'd hoped to send the DNA test off and have the results back before dealing with her again.

"Yeah, she found me. Thanks."

A smattering of applause followed the last chorus of *Jingle Bells*. Mrs. Hoadley grabbed the microphone and spoke over the PA system. "Sylvia...after the children take their bow, do you want them to go to the Green Room or sit out front?"

"I'll be right there," James' mother called back. "Sorry, Jimmy. I've got to go. Next rehearsal is tomorrow night. Show's on Friday. We'll set up the podium for you with a microphone, so you can whisper or put on whatever funny voice you want and it will all carry. You're going to be brilliant."

She kissed his cheek and trotted off, leaving him with the book in his hand and his heart in his mouth. He turned and wandered back down the hall, a piano solo of *I'll be Home for Christmas* pursuing him.

That damn song was following him everywhere.

Chapter Eight

James took a trip to Burlington early the next morning to investigate the original land options for the new Getalot store. He liked traveling—driving with the music on full blast—and today's jaunt provided the perfect opportunity to pick up Christmas gifts for the family along the way.

Like most guys, he hated shopping. Unless it involved cars or electronics. But the Church Street Marketplace in downtown Burlington made the retail experience fun, offering wonderful cafes and a diverse selection of stores and wares. Even in winter, James loved the feel of the open-air mall and the architecture of the area's historic buildings. During the summers, eateries set out tables on the sidewalk and street entertainers performed, while lush trees provided shade as well as beauty.

He found a sweater for his brother, a nifty combination spaghetti measure and trivet for his sister, a personalized cutting board for his parents and a hand-painted silk scarf for Lily. As for Duncan, he'd known exactly what to buy his nephew the first time he'd seen him at the Village Green.

Marcus was a different story.

James tracked through several stores, hoping for inspiration. He finally settled on a round wooden puzzle, a globe of the world and a toy car. James figured Marcus would like spinning the wheels, at least. Making the world go around, too.

He wanted to find something extra special for April, the perfect gift, but nothing leapt out at him. As he searched, he listened to *Pete the Cat Saves Christmas* on his phone using his Bluetooth headset.

He'd found a video of it on YouTube. The story even had a song. He could see why his mother picked it for him to present. The poem was very much like *A Visit from St. Nicholas*. He could use all his performing talents—play the guitar, recite and sing. By the time he left the Marketplace, he had the piece committed to memory.

From Burlington, he headed east to Montpelier, again taking note of the commercial land available for development. Satisfied he'd fully explored the alternatives, he reversed direction and drove back to Carol Falls, thankful he didn't need to stay overnight in a hotel, after all.

He checked his watch. The staff at Billy Boy's should be there by now, getting ready for their afternoon opening. He called and asked to speak to Heather. He wished he could take back the night he'd spent with her, but life didn't work that way, and he couldn't avoid her indefinitely. When he learned she hadn't come in for her shift yet, he left his name and number with a request for a return call.

Errands done, he drove to his brother's house. James admired the Arts and Crafts design and the long porch that stretched across the front of the home. Maybe he'd build one like it for April in the spring.

He knocked and heard heels bounding across the floor. The front door flew open and Duncan appeared, Garret standing right behind him.

"Uncle Jimmy!"

"Hey, Jimbo. What's shakin'?"

"Thought I'd give Santa a hand this year and deliver a few gifts ahead of time."

Garret gestured for him to enter. James stomped the snow off his boots before stepping inside. He dropped his voice. "Is it okay if I give Dunc his present now? I won't be here for Christmas and I want to make sure it's the right fit."

"Not staying for the big day? Mom will be disappointed."

"She already is." James squatted down to Duncan's level. "I've got some things in the trunk of my car. Can you help me bring them in?"

"Sure thing, Uncle Jimmy."

He waited while Duncan put on his coat and boots. They walked the length of the driveway together, James heading to the back of his Porsche. When he popped the trunk, Dunc's face lit up. The boy's unwrapped gifts were front and center—a kid's-sized guitar, along with a case, strap, picks, a capo, extra strings, a tuner and a Beatles T-shirt.

"Do you like 'em?"

"Holy cow! Is that all for me?"

"You bet." Uncles were allowed to spoil their nephews. The excitement on Duncan's face made James feel like a million bucks and proved the old adage. It *was* better to give than to receive.

The little guy held up his arms for a hug. "Will you teach me how to play?"

"We can have a lesson now, if you're not busy." He helped the boy carry in the gifts, Dunc insisting on hauling the guitar himself.

"Dad, look what Uncle Jimmy gave me. And he's going to teach me a song right now."

"That's wonderful." Garret pulled James to one side. "Mind if I leave the two of you on your own? I'd love to have some alone time with Lily. Take her out for an early dinner."

Great idea. One James should replicate. He thought about asking April on a date, but couldn't imagine she'd trust anyone to look after Marcus in her absence. "Sure. Go ahead. Enjoy yourselves."

Garret leveled his gaze, the way he did when he got serious. James braced himself for a reprimand.

"I'm glad you stopped by, Jimmy. Because I wanted to thank you—in person—for taking over the skiing lesson the other day."

James hadn't expected that. "I figured I owed you one after I ruined dinner."

"It was my fault, too. Mom's right. We should be considerate of one another's feelings. And opinions. Particularly at Christmas." Garret clapped him on the back. This time, there was no stiffness. "Remember, no matter what, you'll always be my brother."

James could only nod. He was too choked up to speak. He hoped Garret remembered his promise when the Getalot store moved into town.

After his brother left, James showed Duncan how to tune his new instrument and play a few simple chords. There was lots of eye contact, lots of smiles, and no tantrums. Just a happy, normal kid.

No. Not normal. *Typical.* From his research, James knew parents of autistic children preferred that word. After all, what's *normal?*

Two hours later, Garret was back and Duncan could play the riff from Queen's *Another One Bites the Dust* as well as John Deacon, the song's composer and bass guitarist. James said his good-byes and headed out, feeling like a rock star, too.

April could barely keep the frustration out of her voice. It wasn't her son's fault he was unresponsive to the day's lessons. She was the leader. She was supposed to be the one helping him, and the fact that she wasn't made her more exasperated.

So she gave him paper and crayons and let him draw his favorite shape—circles, of course—while she sought refuge in her pottery, the familiar feel of the wet clay between her fingers.

Even that was a disaster. The set of Christmas mugs she'd made didn't match. No two were the same height, and one had cracked when she fired it in the kiln. Unfortunately, these were the cups she planned to donate to the Baby Holly Fundraising Raffle.

All she could do was try again. Maybe with a different project. A large one, perhaps. Wedging the clay, waking it up and kneading out the air bubbles, would help her take out some of her aggravations.

She sliced off a fist-sized piece of clay from a larger brick and slammed it onto her work table. That felt so good, she hurled another chunk on top of it, where it landed with a satisfying bang.

April loaded all the defeats of the past days when she slammed down the third lump. *The Picnic Fiasco! The Christmas Tree Calamity! The Tobogganing Debacle!*

She remembered Jimmy's hurt over each with the fourth.

Before hurling the fifth, she thought about him walking to his car that morning, his packed bags in his hands. He'd said he'd come back, once he took care of some business.

Would he? After everything she and Marcus had put him through?

In the short time he'd stayed with her, she'd gotten used to having Jimmy around again. Even now, she could smell his cologne, feel his lingering energy. She enjoyed hearing him hum or whistle while he worked—always making music. The silence today had been a small taste of what it would be like when he left.

Permanently.

Muscles sore, she heaved a final piece of clay. It wasn't until she felt Jimmy's arms around her that she knew he'd come in. And that she was crying, his shirt soaking up her tears.

He stepped away, his eyes searching her face. "Are you okay? I saw the lights on in here and..."

"I'm just...*throwing* the clay."

He didn't laugh at her pun, but made a quip of his own. "With that pitch, you should be playing for the Mets."

"I had a little pottery mishap earlier," she explained, disclosing half the truth. "It's nothing."

"Must be something to get this reaction. You're shaking."

April wondered if he'd reach out to her again, hold her. Before he could, Marcus stepped in between them and gave her a hug. Tears welled up again. Happy ones this time.

"You see? Your son's worried about you, too."

She shook her head. "It's more than that. He's giving me a deep compression hug." April closed her eyes and savored the moment. "He's made a connection. I was unhappy and he's trying to make me feel better. It's the biggest emotional breakthrough we've had."

As quickly as the hug began, it stopped. Marcus looked up at the two adults and then whipped around behind Jimmy and pushed him closer to her.

"What's he doing now?"

Marcus clutched one of Jimmy's hands and positioned it on April's hip. He ran to the other side and did the same.

"I think he realizes he's too small to give me the kind of hug I need. He wants you to do it."

"He doesn't need to ask me twice."

Once again, she found herself in Jimmy's arms, held tight against him. It brought back all the memories, all the longings. She felt like one of those jigsaw pieces in her classroom, finally reunited with its mate.

Snug together. Perfectly aligned.

Marcus pressed against the backs of her legs, holding her too. She stood there sandwiched between her two favorite boys.

Make that *three* boys. Bandit rubbed up against her shins, his tail patting her as if to say, 'There, there.'

When the last of her sobs ebbed, Jimmy led her over to the table with the crayons. He sat beside her, his arm draped across her shoulders. "You sure you're okay?"

"Much better."

"I hope you know, I'm here for you April. I want to help you and Marcus in any way I can." Jimmy gazed at her son, watching as the boy went back to drawing circles. "How long has he been getting therapy? From what I've heard, early intervention is important."

"Unfortunately, Marcus didn't receive it." A reality which broke her heart. "Before I adopted him, his therapy was sporadic at best."

"Why is that?"

"He was shuffled between families for years. While I was teaching, our paths kept crossing. I'd see him for a while, make some progress and then he'd be gone, sent to live with different people."

New tears formed in her eyes. She blinked and turned away so Jimmy wouldn't see them. "When he came to me this last time, I decided to give him a real home. My heart just went out to him because he reminded me so much of..."

You.

But she couldn't admit that to Jimmy. Like Marcus, he'd seemed apart from the world. Adrift, anchorless. And in her son's hazel eyes, she'd seen her childhood sweetheart all over again, and his desperate need to belong. She couldn't have turned Marcus away, no matter what. It would have broken her heart.

"Myself," she said, instead.

"Well...while I'm here, let me do what I can for both of you."

That was the key phrase. While he was here. He didn't plan on sticking around. And she'd already become too attached to him. Was already falling in love.

All over again.

James kept his expression neutral but, on the inside, he was smiling. Marcus had wanted him to hug April. Had insisted on it, by pushing them together.

It was a small step in getting Marcus to accept him, but James felt lighter, happier and, even though it was premature, he felt hope for the future.

A future with April.

He started making plans. If Stephen chose April's land for the Getalot store, they could all stay right here while James supervised the building. If the new outlet ended up elsewhere, April and Marcus could come with him, and stay in a hotel near the site.

James frowned. That last option sounded great for him but terrible for everyone else. Marcus wouldn't have any place to play and the poor kid would be uprooted again. Plus, April would have to abandon her school idea.

"Why don't I start by helping you clean up that clay?" James asked, trying to think of a plan that didn't involve the three of them living in two different locations. He held out his hand to April and she took it, hers small and fragile in his. That simple touch made his chest swell with pure joy.

"Marcus?" As usual, the boy ignored him. James glanced over the child's shoulder and froze. He blinked, unbelieving. He turned to April and registered her expression, likely a mirror image of his own—eyes big, mouth open in surprise.

On the table in front of Marcus lay a drawing of an angel, looking exactly like the one James made in the snow.

April let out an excited, high-pitched squeak, her eyes sparkling. She wrapped her arms around her son and gave him a kiss. "Good drawing, Marcus. Good angel."

"Hey, don't *I* get a kiss? I was the model for the picture, after all," James joked.

"Okay. But only one."

He didn't think she'd take the bait. Now that she had...

She drew closer, her mouth en route to his cheek. At the last minute, he turned his head, so their lips met.

Hers were soft, warm, sweet. He could have stayed like that for the next hour, tasting her, drinking her in. But a moment later, his cell phone jangled. The alarm he'd set to remind himself of his mother's rehearsal.

He pulled the device from his pocket to turn it off and get back to kissing, but there was a call coming through. Thinking it might be Stephen on the other end, James answered, prepared to ditch the guy ASAP.

"I need to see you." It was a woman's voice. One he didn't recognize.

"Who is this?"

"Heather. Heather Connolly."

Parts of him shriveled at the sound of her name. "Okay. When and where?"

"Now. At the bar."

He could only assume she meant Billy Boy's. "Fine. I'm leaving right away." He hung up and shoved the phone into his pocket.

"When will you be back?" April dipped her head. "Sorry. None of my business."

"Of course, it's your business." He slipped a finger under her chin to raise it. He hovered there, looking at her lips, pink and moist. If he stopped to kiss her now, he'd never quit. "Let me take care of this and I'll be back as soon as I can."

"I'll see you later then."

"Later," he promised, and forced himself to walk out the door.

She couldn't believe they'd kissed.

It had been everything she'd remembered. *Better*. But not all that she'd wanted. That would involve him making a trip to her bedroom later in the night.

Which would be a mistake.

They weren't those people anymore. And there was nothing holding Jimmy to Carol Falls. However long he planned on staying, it wouldn't be enough time. Not for April. If she let things get out of hand, she'd end up nursing a bruised heart, if not a broken one.

So what the heck had he been thinking, kissing her like that? Getting her all worked up and hopeful?

Darn him, anyhow.

His phone had interrupted them just in time. Now hers was ringing. You'd think she was running a Santa Hotline with the calling frenzy. Her heart leapt when she saw the name 'Frost' on the screen, and then she realized it wasn't Jimmy's name, but Sylvia's.

His mother.

April hadn't talked to the woman for years, and was hesitant to do so now. Jimmy's mom had always been pleasant, but so well-spoken, so perfectly put together all the time, that April had felt a little intimidated by her.

"Hello, Mrs. Frost."

There was a slight pause on the other end, during which April could hear piano music and murmurs of conversation in the background.

"Goodness, April. How did you know it was me? Oh, yes. Your phone would have told you. These little gadgets are amazing, aren't they?" Another music-filled break.

"I hope you don't mind me calling. I got your number from Mrs. Hoadley. I hear you're taking a shift selling raffle tickets at the recital. It'll be lovely to see you again. Maybe we can go for coffee together one day soon."

April was sure Mrs. Frost hadn't called to invite her for a jolt of caffeine. And wouldn't that meeting be interesting? How many women had coffee with their ex-mother-in-law? When there were no grandchildren involved?

"That would be nice, Mrs. Frost."

"Please, call me Sylvia."

"All right...Sylvia. Is there something I can do for you?" *Stop seeing your son, for instance?*

"Actually, I'm looking for Jimmy. We're having a rehearsal for the Winter Recital and he's going to give a reading."

Ah, so that's what he'd run off to do. Odd that he'd said nothing about it.

April explained that Jimmy was on his way and probably hadn't picked up his phone because he was driving.

"Oh, good. I was worried he'd forgotten."

Which was totally like Jimmy, at least, in the old days, and one of the reasons her parents didn't like her choice for a boyfriend. They'd dubbed him *Mr. Unreliable*, mostly for his habit of skipping classes, and cautioned April to protect her heart. To stay aloof.

Still good advice considering Jimmy would skip town before the weekend was through. Hoping a man with wanderlust would settle down was foolhardy at best. She'd be better off pinning her hopes to more predictable outcomes. Like winning the lottery.

No matter how attractive Jimmy was, no matter how much she felt that old pull, she wasn't prepared to gamble away her heart.

Chapter Nine

James scanned Billy Boy's Bar and Pool Hall. Apart from the
addition of a few tired Christmas wreaths hanging in the windows,
it hadn't changed since the last time he was here.

The time that changed everything.

As the name implied, this was a man's bar, designed for serious
drinkers. The lighting was dim, so you could hide if you wanted. The
bar was long, because alcohol was the main thing on the menu. The
kitchen's specialities were slim and high in caloric intake—burgers,
fries, chili—nothing fancy, just greasy deliciousness.

Some claimed the waitresses were even tastier, all tall, blonde
and buxom. Their black dresses were low in the neck and high on the
thigh—Barbie wannabes balanced precariously on five-inch stilettos.

Heather Connolly had been one of them.

Now she sat at a table in the far corner, wearing a long bib
apron. Was she working in the kitchen now?

On his way over to her, James passed Zack, the bouncer, and
heard a clatter as someone made a shot on a nearby pool table. James
did a double take. One of the guys playing was the town's mayor,
Emerson Lincoln. He wore a fancy suit—almost as fine as his
McMansion. The man with him looked pretty rich, too. Maybe it was
true what they said about the bar, that more deals were made here
than in offices.

A strong hand grabbed James around his bicep. Only one guy in
the place had a grip like that. James turned to face him. "What can I
do for you, Zack?"

"You here to see Heather?"

"That a problem?"

"Not unless you make it one. She's been through a lot, our
Heather. Last guy who was with her cleaned out her bank account
and broke her jaw."

James winced in sympathy. So that's why she looked different.

"The jerk messed up her heart worse," Zack added.

Whoever patched her up hadn't done such a great job either, but she'd certainly gained an ally in the bouncer. If she'd wanted a watch dog, Zack was the perfect breed. The pit bull variety. James had never seen the tough guy so protective. Maybe the staff here took care of one another. Zack had referred to her as 'our' Heather.

"I'm here because she asked me to meet her."

Zack released his arm, but stretched up to his full height, making eye contact with James' chin. "Okay then, Jimmy. Let's not keep the lady waiting."

Empty peanut shells crackled under James' boots as he continued alone to Heather's table. She had a beer in front of her, hardly touched. James took a seat beside her so they could talk over Kid Rock's *Bawitdaba* without shouting.

"Wanna drink?"

He shook his head. He'd already learned that lesson. And he didn't think April would appreciate him coming back to her smelling of booze. Not after what happened to her parents.

"You wanted to see me, Heather?"

"Sorry I called you away from...whatever you were doing."

"That's okay," he said. Though it wasn't. "I was with my..." What could he call April? His ex-wife? His soul mate? "My girlfriend," he said, at last.

"The one who wrote you that letter?"

James jerked upright, and then covered his reaction by shifting in his chair. "What do you know about the letter?"

She gave him a sad smile. "You really don't remember much about that night you crashed at my place. You were upset after your dad's party. You were talking about it, while we knocked back a few. And then you mentioned this letter a girl named April sent you a long time ago. I take it you've reconnected with her." Heather flinched, as she'd done when he'd met her at Kate's. Almost imperceptibly, but it was there.

"Is your jaw bothering you?"

She wrapped her arms around herself. "Did Zack tell you? For a big macho guy, he's an awful blabbermouth."

"Your ex hurt you?"

"Yes. After he...found out about us."

With that news, James was ready to join Team Zack and protect

Heather, too. "I'm sorry."

She gazed at her glass, ran her hands over the condensation, her fingers glistening in the soft light.

"So...why did you want to see me, Heather?"

"Have you told your sister about me?"

"No. Why?"

"She's a cop and I heard they might press charges against Holly's mother."

"I think they're more concerned that you get medical treatment. Have you seen a doctor?"

"No. I—"

"You need to get checked out."

"I don't have the money for that, James. And I'm fine, really. I've always been pretty healthy." She wiped her wet fingers on the apron.

"You're working in the kitchen?"

"Yeah. The boss was nice enough to keep me on, though I wouldn't be good on the floor now. Not with my smile messed up...and the baby weight. I miss the tips but at least it's something. And Kate's letting me do mornings at her cafe. I get a discount on food at both places, so that helps. I'm about to have dinner now that my shift's over. Want to join me?"

"No thanks, but you go ahead." James waved at a waitress, who could have been the old Heather's twin. "Could I get a coffee? And what would you like, Heather? My treat."

"You don't have to buy me—"

"I want to. How 'bout a burger?"

She shook her head. "Too hard to chew."

"The chili, then?"

"Sure. That would be great. And a chocolate milkshake, please." Heather's cheeks glowed. "I got a little too fond of those when I had my jaw problems."

"Coming right up." The waitress turned on her mile-high heels and clomped back to the bar.

Feeding Heather would ease his conscience. He could settle up the bill and leave her to her dinner. "You drive here?"

"Walked."

"It's dark and cold. And this isn't the best neighborhood."

She shrugged. "Cars are expensive to run. Plus walking will help me get back in shape."

"Not tonight." He'd see her home safely. It was the least he could do.

"Thanks for being nice to me." When she looked up from her beer, her eyes were glazed with tears. "I know this was my fault. I don't usually pick up men in bars, please know that, James." She clutched his arm, and then seemed embarrassed by the contact and returned her hand to her glass. "It's just that you were so sweet, and looked so unhappy, and my heart..."

She choked up, took a swig of beer and set the glass back down on the table. Her hands, unoccupied, fluttered nervously. "I'd been on and off with my ex for a while, so I wasn't on the pill. I should have been thinking ahead about protection, but I hadn't expected things to...well...go as far as they did. I guess..."

Heather fiddled with one of the large hoop earrings she wore. "I guess we just needed each other that night. And...I couldn't help it...but I fell a little bit in love with you."

The waitress reappeared with James' coffee. He wondered how much she'd heard. As soon as she was gone, he leaned forward, so he could talk quietly and still be understood.

"I'm sorry if you feel I led you on, but I've—"

"You've got a girlfriend. I get it."

Heather's chili and milkshake arrived. He kept her company while she ate. She seemed reluctant to chow down in front of him and he had to encourage her to have more. She managed to eat half.

"Now, let's get you home." He grabbed the coat draped on the back of her chair and held it for her. She slipped into it, thanking him. James shrugged into his own jacket and reached for his wallet. He threw some bills on the table—more than enough to cover the drinks, the meal and a tip—and escorted Heather to the exit.

Mayor Lincoln, tall and fit like a Kennedy stand-in, glanced up from his scotch. "Nice car, Frost."

"Glad you like it, Emerson." James tipped his imaginary hat at the dignitary, and played the gentleman to Heather, holding the door open for her. On the ride to her place, they didn't talk. He listened to the radio and she played with her earring.

When they reached her place, he walked her up to her apartment. She invited him in and opened the door wide, but he said his farewells, took her hand and placed a bunch of twenties in it.

"Oh, James. I can't."

"I've had people help me when I needed it. This is my turn. Besides...it's Christmas."

James spied a foot-high, decorated tree through the open door. The rest of the apartment looked pretty much the same as he recalled—a bachelor suite with a small kitchenette and a couch. During his previous, booze-hazed visit, he hadn't noticed the details. He did now—from the tired yellow paint to the few balls of wool sitting on the couch.

"I couldn't do much while I was recuperating," she explained. "I taught myself how to knit. I figured I could make people scarves for Christmas."

He saw some framed photos on the wall by the door—several of Heather, the way he remembered her from before, but mostly shots of a fair-haired girl about Duncan's age.

"Who's that?"

"My daughter, Charlotte. She was visiting with my sister when you and I..."

James looked around for evidence of a child. A couple of drawings were posted on the refrigerator but there wasn't a toy in sight. "She's not with you now?"

"Not after what happened with Chase." Heather touched her jaw for a moment, and then stroked Charlotte's image. "Child Services took her. I'm trying to get her back. Once we're together— you, me and the baby—they'll know everything's stable. They'll return Charlotte then."

James backed away, the doorjamb digging into his spine. "Together?"

"I mean, when they see you stepping up. Acknowledging the baby. You *are* going to step up, right?"

"If she's mine." Again, she flinched, as if he'd hurt her. "I know you've been through a lot, Heather, and I don't mean to doubt you, but I need to be sure."

"Of course. Did you want me to take a DNA test?"

"I don't think that's necessary. I'll get myself compared to Holly. That should be enough."

"You haven't done it yet?"

"No. I just received the kit yesterday."

She let out a sigh "Good. It's good that you make sure, James."

Her easy acceptance left him with a niggling feeling that she was telling the truth, that her child was his.

Heather thanked him again and gave him a teary hug. By the time his brain registered that he should return it, she'd closed the door and he was left standing in the hallway, alone.

April saw Jimmy's headlights turn into the drive. She passed another ten minutes tidying the living room and wondered what was taking him so long to come in. When she went to the window and pulled back the drape, she could see his dark outline in the driver's seat.

What was he doing out there?

Finally, the car's interior light snapped on. He got out and walked around to the trunk, retrieving several items. Thinking she could help, she grabbed her coat and went outside.

"How'd rehearsal go?"

He looked at her as if through a fog. "Rehearsal?"

"Your mom called here wondering where you were. Did you arrive late?"

Jimmy hung his head. "Damn. I missed it. Something else came up."

Something that kept him sitting in his car for ten minutes mulling it over. But she wasn't going to ask. If he wanted to confide in her, he would.

Instead of talking, he loaded his arms with three items, and almost dropped one.

"Let me help you with that." She reached out and found herself holding a toy car.

"For Marcus," he said.

His thoughtfulness touched her, made her smile. "Thanks. Anything else I can carry?"

"I picked up some cream for our morning coffee. It's in the front seat, if you can grab it." Meanwhile, he moved the Christmas tree on the porch a foot closer to the door, his ongoing experiment to help Marcus accept it.

April reached into the car to claim the bag. On the floor in front of it, something glittered.

"Are you practicing to be a pirate?" she asked, stooping to retrieve the item that caught her eye. She held the hoop earring up to the light.

Jimmy blanched. "I gave a girl a ride home. It was cold and——"

April fought the slow burn spreading through her chest. She had no right to be jealous. "You don't owe me any explanations, Jimmy."

"But I want to explain."

"You gave a girl a ride home, and as she was sitting in the car, her gold hoop just slipped out of her ear. Sure thing. Happens to me all the time."

"April, please——"

"You need a place to stay and I need some work done on the house. That's it, Jimmy. There's nothing else holding us together. Don't sweat it. I'm not."

The car door got away from her and she ended up slamming it. So much for trying to appear aloof. She was about to retreat into the house when the glow of two more headlights came bouncing up the drive. A little late for an unannounced visitor to pay a social call.

The white truck came to a stop and April recognized the Frost Farms logo on the side of it. This was Garret's vehicle, and a visit from Jimmy's brother at this time of night could mean only one thing.

Trouble.

Chapter Ten

The roar of the engine died and another roar replaced it. A baby's wail.

When Garret opened his driver's side door, the howls reached a crescendo. Certainly, the kid had been born with a good set of lungs.

"Hi, Garret," James said, surprised by his brother's late night visit. "How's it going?"

"Loudly. Mom's been trying to lull this little one to sleep for an hour. I thought a car ride might do the trick but..."

Garret slid open the back door and James could now see, as well as *hear*, Holly—her face pinched, her tiny tongue quivering as she yowled. Garret exchanged shouted pleasantries with April, before turning back to James.

"I got as far as the covered bridge and thought about you out here, Jimmy. You and your golden throat. A lullaby might be worth a try."

"You don't know any lullabies, Garret?" April asked.

"If the kid heard me sing, she'd probably cry harder."

"I don't know if that's possible," she joked back. "Look, why don't we take her tonight. Give you guys a break."

"That would be great. If you're sure you don't mind."

When April said she'd be happy to help out, James agreed to the plan. How could he refuse? From day one, Garret and the family had been caring for the baby. Possibly *his* baby. He should have stepped up without being asked.

More selfishly, now that Holly was here, he'd be able to take her sample cheek swab in privacy.

"Thanks, April. Thanks, Jimmy." And, just like that, Garret plunked the tot in James' arms.

He knew how to hold an infant, how to support its head and cup its bottom, how to cradle a child near his body, to provide warmth, comfort and safety. But he kept Holly an inch away, feeling awkward with the baby. He didn't even have the strength to correct Garret on his name and say *James*, and barely said goodbye to him before he drove off. All he could do was gaze down at the poor kid, sobs pouring out of her mouth, her cheeks red with the effort.

Inside the house, James searched Holly's face for his own features, as he made tracks to his room off the kitchen. Did she have his nose? His eyes? Bawling like she was now, she didn't look much like anyone. Maybe a red-faced politician.

Garret had brought over supplies with the baby, which April helped James juggle—the child's carrier, bottles of formula, extra diapers, powder. After checking to see if she was wet (no) or hungry (absolutely not), rocking her seemed the next order of business. James struck out at that, as well.

"Do you think she's ill?" April asked.

James kissed the baby's forehead. "She's not hot, so I don't think she has a fever."

Looked like a serenade was in order. Someone once said, music could soothe the savage beast. James hoped it would have the same effect on a *baby* beast, since he had to practice for the recital.

He slipped Holly into her carrier, setting it on the floor so he could rock her with his foot while both of his hands were occupied with his guitar. While the baby howled, James quickly figured out the chords of the *Pete the Cat* song and began to play and sing.

April sat on the bed. And wherever April went, Marcus and Bandit followed. The cat jumped on the comforter, curled into a ball and closed his eyes. The boy dragged along his magnetic board and letters, setting them up beside his mom.

"I'm surprised you didn't pursue a career in music," April said, after a few minutes.

"It's a tough industry. I wasn't good enough."

"You were. You *are*."

"Thanks for thinking so." He'd missed having her as his number one fan. As he repeated the song, perfecting his fingering and experimenting with the tempo, Marcus approached.

James tried to keep his excitement in check—a captivated ten-year-old and a baby who was nodding off—maybe he did have some magic when it came to kids, after all. Then he realized, Marcus was more interested in the baby than the music.

James knew the boy enjoyed seeing things spin, like April's

potter's wheel. Maybe the rocking attracted him.

April gravitated to her son's side. "As far as I know, he's never been around a newborn," she told James. "Gentle," she said softly, coaching Marcus.

The boy paused and then knelt at the baby's feet. He stayed there motionless for several minutes and then flopped down on his belly, his head propped up on his fists, so he was almost eye level with the little girl.

James and April looked at each other, and then back to the boy. Something was happening. Marcus was truly fascinated with the baby, when normally he wasn't interested in people at all.

Then Marcus began to hum.

James was so astonished, he stopped playing, but Marcus didn't seem to notice. He kept humming for the baby, repeating the melody he'd just heard James play.

Tears gathered in April's eyes, but she didn't move. Nor did James. They didn't want to do anything to ruin the moment.

Then, in her sleep, the baby yawned. That broke the spell. Marcus sat back on his heels, rose and walked away, retreating into his own world again, as if nothing had happened.

April made a mental note to get her eyes checked. They were leaking again. This habit of bursting into tears whenever Marcus made a connection had to stop.

"Sorry to be such a blubber-puss," she said, wiping her eyes with the heels of her hands.

From her watery peripheral vision, she saw James set his guitar aside. A moment later, he was stroking her back. "You're entitled. That was amazing."

Why did his touch feel so good, so right? How was it that the warmth of him melted away the years, leaving her comforted while longing for more?

She turned to look at him and found herself enfolded in his arms. She tugged at the front of his shirt, making him bend to her until their lips met. This was what she needed—what she'd *always* needed. And, from the way he moaned into her mouth, the way his heart hammered against her palms, she knew he wanted it, too—that her suspicions about another woman in his life were unfounded.

He broke off the kiss too soon, before she'd had her fill. Still, he held her—tighter than before—as if afraid to let her go.

"You kiss me like you mean it, April. You make me—" His voice was hoarse, his breathing rough.

"I make you...what?"

"Scared."

She pulled away slightly, enough so she could see his eyes. The Jimmy she'd known wasn't afraid of anything. Not the tallest ski jump or the wildest horse.

"Scared of what?"

His jaw tightened. She smoothed her hand over it. "Tell me," she whispered.

He glanced past her, probably checking on Marcus. In the silence she could hear her son playing with his plastic letters. And she had a clear view of the baby, still sleeping peacefully in the carrier. April was about to repeat her question, when Jimmy finally spoke.

"That your parents were right. That I wasn't good enough for you. That one day you'd figure it out too, and leave me again."

Dear God. Did he think she'd had a choice all those years ago? "I didn't want to leave, Jimmy. My parents forced me."

"But you agreed to the annulment."

She had. That much was true. And she'd explained why in the letter he'd never received, never read. "They threatened me, said they'd charge you with kidnapping for taking me to Vegas."

His gaze shot to her face. A furrow appeared between his brows, the one that used to surface whenever he was shocked or worried. In the old days, she'd kiss it away. She wondered what he'd do if she tried that now. If she stretched up on her tiptoes and pressed her lips against his forehead.

Would he let her? Would he think she was crazy?

She took a chance and did it, feeling the anxiety ease from his body before she continued her story. "I told them I'd wanted to go, that I planned the trip. They wouldn't listen. They said they'd see you behind bars before they'd accept our marriage."

Jimmy's shoulders slumped. "Wow. They really hated me."

"No. It was never about you. It was about *me*. And their need for control."

She hugged her man close. "I didn't understand it when I was younger. I understand it now that I'm a mother. They thought they were being good parents, protecting me. And, in a way, they were.

But they forced the issue. We'd never have considered getting married so young, if my parents had tried, just a little, to understand how we felt about each other. Instead, they reacted with anger, because I'd defied them. They hurt me...and I hurt you...and I'm sorry, Jimmy. Truly, truly sorry."

He let out a sigh, his hands slipping to her waist. "You keep kissing me and I'm going to feel much better real soon."

She laughed and planned to kiss him until they were both breathless, but then she noticed the letters on Marcus' board.

April wrapped her arm around Jimmy, dragging him over to take a better look. The sight in front of her made her freeze to the spot. Marcus had positioned his plastic letters to form a word. She rested her hand on her chest, fresh tears gathering in her eyes.

"*Ba...by,*" Jimmy said, drawing out each syllable, just as she did when she was teaching Marcus.

"What about the baby, my darling?"

Marcus looked at the board. Slowly, he picked out different letters from the pile on the bedspread. When he was finished, April read the words aloud.

"Smells nice."

Chapter Eleven

At breakfast, Marcus was still spelling words. Better than James could at that age. Although he'd done nothing to help Marcus learn, he felt a wave of pride for the boy.

Rocking Holly in his arms, James thought he might just be ready for parenthood. He'd had to get up during the night for feedings and was a little tired, but seeing the two kids doing so well energized him more than a nap ever could.

Good thing, because he had a busy day ahead. Dropping off Holly at Frost Farms was at the front of it, the Winter Recital at the tail end—and he'd already assured his mother he would be there, on time, ready to perform.

In between, he needed to mail off the DNA samples he'd taken, buy supplies to fix the bathroom ceiling and pick up Marcus' special food at Kate's. After some initial hesitation, it turned out the little guy liked the new things she'd prepared.

He arrived at the cafe later that morning and spotted Heather wiping a table, Kate nowhere to be found. Excellent timing. He sure didn't want an audience for this confrontation.

James pulled the earring from his pocket. "I believe this is yours."

"Thank goodness. Where did you find it?"

"I didn't. My girlfriend did. In my car."

Heather flushed. "Oh, James. I'm sorry. I hope I didn't make trouble for you." She was so genuinely apologetic and embarrassed that he felt guilty for suspecting her of leaving the earring in his vehicle on purpose.

"Was that who you were visiting the other day out on Tamarack Tree Lane?"

Though she'd been repentant, he didn't want to give her any more information than necessary. And he certainly didn't want to involve April in any of this.

"I'm sorry if it sounded like I was accusing you. Finding the earring was just...a very awkward moment."

"I completely understand. If there's anything I can do to make it up to you..."

"That's okay." Her eagerness for penance only made him feel guiltier. He softened his voice. "How are you managing?"

"Much better, thanks to you."

"You've got enough money?"

"I'm fine." But she said the words quickly, leading him to believe her situation was far from fine.

"Did you need more?"

"No, no. Actually, what I need is...some moral support." Heather raked her top teeth over her bottom lip. "I was wondering if you'd come to the police station with me. Once I work up the courage to tell them the truth."

His stomach took a dive. Accompanying her would pretty much look like an admission of guilt. "We'll talk about it, when you're ready. Did you drive here?"

"I walked again. I'm going to the Winter Recital this evening and, since it's just down the street, I didn't need to bring the car." She smiled shyly. "I hear you're performing."

"That's right. Hope you enjoy it."

He slipped her a few extra bucks for a cab home following the show and she left soon afterward, her shift at Kate's done for the day.

James sat and waited for Marcus' food, sipping coffee. His phone buzzed and he viewed the text message—Stephen's offer on April's farm. James' initial excitement diminished as he read the amount again. It was much lower than he'd suggested. He'd do what he could to talk Stephen into going higher, but at least now he had an offer on the table. He couldn't wait to tell April about it.

He pulled up to the farm an hour later. There was another vehicle already in the driveway that he had to squeeze in beside. A car he recognized.

His heart sank. What was Heather doing here?

The front door opened and she emerged. When she reached the walkway, he blocked her path. "What's going on?"

Her cheeks reddened. "I-I-I heard April makes pottery. I wondered if she had any Christmas pieces for sale. Did I do wrong?"

She flipped her hair back as she spoke, exposing those hoop earrings. If April noticed them...

"I'm sure you were just trying to be nice, Heather, but I don't want you here." That came out harsh. Still, he needed to make his boundaries clear. "If you have to reach me, you've got my number."

She took a step back, her hand lifting defensively. "Okay, James. Okay. I'll stay away."

Her stricken expression had him feeling guilty all over again. Had he misread her? At least, she got in her car and headed back to town. However hard it was to deal with her, he figured explaining to April was going to be far worse.

He retrieved Marcus' food from his trunk and let himself in the front door, pulling it closed with his foot.

"April?" He called her name again but no one answered. When he went into the kitchen to put the take-out in the fridge, he found her sitting at the table, the cat at her feet. Bandit's tail sliced the air as he gave James a cold stare. April looked just as grim.

"Why was there a Getalot man here surveying my land? I asked him, but he said I should speak to you."

Yes. Far worse.

James put the groceries away, stealing an extra minute to pull himself together. He thought about sitting, but the chair across from her looked too much like a *hot seat*. He remained standing.

"Getalot hires me as an independent contractor, to look at land options and oversee new constructions. That's why I'm in the area. To check out proposed locations for a Vermont store. You said you'd had this place up for sale, and I know it would be a great spot for the franchise. For you, too. If you wanted to sell the whole farm, you could take the money and set up your school in a more central area. Or, you could keep the house and the barn. The Getalot store would be right next door. How convenient is that?"

Although, as he said it, it didn't sound convenient at all. He pictured the tree with their initials—the only one left standing—smack dab in the parking lot, where it would eventually wither and die. He pictured Marcus running out in the street, into the added traffic, and getting hurt. He saw the school through April's eyes. There'd be no place for the kids to play. Not like the two of them had—running through the sugarwood, breathing in the clean mountain air, enjoying the freedom of youth.

He thought back to the argument he'd had with Garret and, for the life of him, James couldn't remember now what he'd been defending. Concrete and asphalt?

No. *Jobs. Jobs and opportunity.*

"Look, there's a real need in this community for a Getalot store. People want to work. And they want to stretch every dollar they earn." He found himself repeating the narration of a Getalot training video, April looking at him as if he'd just turned into a two-headed ogre. Didn't she get it? "Your own parents objected to me because they thought I had no future. Getalot gave me one. I made something of myself. I'm different now."

April had never seen Jimmy so vehement, his chest heaving, his voice echoing off the walls. And she couldn't take another word. She slammed her hands on the table, as she stood and met his gaze.

"I appreciate the fact that you've improved yourself. But you don't need to change who you are at heart to be acceptable. The Jimmy I knew was a great guy. You're still that person. Look at all you've done for me. You're kind and generous and this Getalot thing...it's just not who you are."

"You don't think I'm capable of holding down a high-powered job?"

Now she'd insulted him, and she hadn't meant to. She softened her delivery. "You can do anything you set your mind to do. You've proven that. I just don't think you'll be happy working for a big corporation like that long term, Jimmy."

He hooked his thumbs into his belt, his glare boring into her.

"Well, I am. And it's *James.*"

Chapter Twelve

After the drama, April drove herself and Marcus to the school, so she could start her shift selling raffle tickets in the makeshift booth just outside the doors of the gym auditorium. She needed some space, some distance, some time away to sort through the argument with Jimmy.

Correction, *James.*

She didn't want them to part on a bad note, but maybe it was better this way. Otherwise, she'd end up pining for him after he left. And probably would anyway.

She put all that aside and donned her happy face, ready to greet customers. The huge prize basket was on the table in front of her, the contents ranging from Kate's jelly preserves and Sylvia's homemade maple cookies, to April's own Christmas mugs—a second batch she'd produced. All proceeds were going to a fund for baby Holly, in addition to the clothes, toys and diapers folks had purchased on their own to donate.

April couldn't imagine living in a more generous community than Carol Falls. They'd printed 2,000 tickets, believing the number to be wishful thinking. *Au contraire.* Mrs. Hoadley had already made one trip to the school office to print another 500. And it looked like they were on the verge of selling out again. At two dollars a pop, Holly would be on her way to a bright future.

If only April's future with Jimmy was as brilliant.

She smoothed out the huge, red cloth they'd thrown over the table for display, and straightened out the books of tickets, making sure there was a pen ready at each station. Then she peered underneath the cloth to check on Marcus, who'd made a little nest for himself beneath the table and was playing with the toy car Jimmy bought him, spinning its wheels.

"Hi, April."

April dropped the cloth and straightened, ready to deliver her sales pitch. But the tall, blonde woman in front of her appeared troubled, agitated.

"Did you want to buy a raffle ticket, Heather?"

"No thanks. Actually...I want to talk to you."

Jimmy sweated under his collar as he tuned his guitar. He hadn't played in front of a group for a while and had a huge case of performance jitters, the kind that made his belly feel as if he were riding a rollercoaster.

The fact that things had gone sideways with April didn't help.

He knew she was still angry with him when she'd driven to the school on her own. He'd tried to apologize but it sounded dead on his tongue. He'd spent most of his adult life trying to better himself, to be the man Mr. and Mrs. Rochester had expected for their daughter. It was hard to let that go.

But, without April, what did any of it matter?

With his guitar strapped to his back, he walked from the dressing rooms, through the halls to the front lobby, determined to speak to her. All the way, he could hear the performance going on inside the gymnasium. Piano music played *Let it Snow* and, judging by the amount of clacking going on, a dance troupe was tapping to it, their footfalls sounding like synchronized rain on a steel roof.

But not everyone was watching the performance. He could see Marcus in the middle of the hall, spinning. Three older kids gathered in an alcove, just below a plaque that James knew displayed the school's motto, 'Only what we give remains our own.'

The boys pointed at Marcus and laughed. In between their snickers, James picked up a few words. *Useless. Stupid. Retard-o.*

He approached the boys, letting his disgust show on his face. "You know what that plaque says?" When the kids gave him blank stares he explained the old, 'I'm rubber, you're glue' concept, and that calling people names only reflected badly on the name-caller. At the end of his diatribe, he told them to get back in the auditorium. As they gawped at him open-mouthed, he added, "Now."

They scattered like mice, scurrying away from sight.

James broke into a trot, needing to get to April, to know things were okay between them. But then he saw her expression—her face drawn and pale, except for the redness creeping into her cheeks. She'd seen the boys, too. Had been on her way to rescue Marcus when James intervened. He didn't register the person standing beside her until a second later.

Heather Connolly.

Dread cemented him to the spot. He could only assume Heather had told April about the baby. Not Heather's fault. He should have stepped up and confessed to April himself. Then he could have avoided this situation entirely.

He strode over to them, Heather running down the hall and out the front doors ahead of him.

"April...I can explain."

"It's too late for that."

Oh, God. Wasn't she going to give him a chance? "But April..."

"There's no time. That's your cue."

He cocked an ear to the auditorium. She was right. He could hear Mrs. Hoadley introducing him.

"I don't care about the show. All I care about is you and Marcus."

"Well, your mom cares about the show. And I know you don't want to let her down. So go. Get up there and perform."

"Not until you give me a chance to explain."

She threw her hands up in the air. "You don't need to say a word, Jimmy. Actually, I'd prefer you didn't. Because when you out and out lie to me...when you share personal things between us with a stranger..."

"Who? Heather? I didn't talk to her about us." He reached for her arm but she pulled away.

"You told her about the letter I sent you. You *did* receive it. You knew about it all along and lied to me. If you didn't want to be with me then, why should I think you'd want to be with me now? I've been such a fool to believe in you."

From the door of the auditorium, James' mother called to him in a loud stage whisper. "Jimmy—I need you now."

Mrs. Hoadley was filling in with an impromptu attempt at stand-up that proved comedy wasn't as easy as it looked. The audience was getting restless and voiced it with a low murmur of disapproval.

"I'll be right back, April. And then, we'll talk." He stepped away from her, his hand outstretched. "Stay here. *Please.* Stay right here."

James had planned to make his entrance from backstage. Since he was already near the doors to the auditorium, he entered and ran up the center aisle with his guitar, taking his place at the podium, in front of the open book.

He'd been ready for this, learned the story inside out. Now, he couldn't remember one word. All he could think about was that scene in the lobby and April's expression.

He scanned the audience, feeling the same way he used to when asked to read aloud—his stomach roiling, his hands shaking, the sweat pouring out of him.

"Hi, I'm James..."

He paused, looking into the faces of the people before him. Some he didn't know. Most he did. Though he hadn't seen them in years, he still recognized them. And there in the front row was his family—his parents, Joey, Garret and Duncan. Lily Parker sat beside his brother holding baby Holly and, right behind her was Kate.

"Jimmy," he corrected. "I'm Jimmy Frost. And my mother asked me here today to read a book she thought everyone would enjoy." He announced the title and the crowd clapped and cheered. Score one for his mom.

In rehearsal, he'd marked the beginning of the story with a chord on his guitar. He hit it and then his gaze fell to the three sneering boys he'd caught earlier. He scanned past the auditorium and spied April in the hallway, dressed in her coat and hat, kneeling in front of Marcus and coaxing him into his winter jacket.

Ready to leave.

Now, Jimmy really started to sweat. He couldn't let her go. Not like this.

He remembered something his grandmother once told him, that life wasn't a dress rehearsal. It was happening—right here, right now. And he had nothing more to lose.

He cleared his throat. "When my mother said she wanted me to stand up here in front of you all and read...I was scared." Turned out he was afraid of adlibbing on the spot, too. His knees knocked together.

"I've always avoided reading aloud. Mrs. Hoadley can tell you that. I tried every trick in the book to get out of it, even cut class. I was always afraid the other kids would make fun of me, because my reading was so bad."

Folks in the seats started nudging each other, realizing this part of the act wasn't planned. Jimmy plowed on.

"What seemed so easy for everyone else was really hard for me. I didn't know what was wrong then but, over the years, I figured it out."

He paused, half-hoping for a power outage, or a small tornado—anything to interrupt his speech. Jimmy took a breath and manned up.

"I have dyslexia."

A rumble of voices rippled through the room. His mother looked anguished, his dad horrified. April stopped dressing Marcus and turned her eyes to the stage.

"I was so worried about appearing stupid that I didn't tell anyone or ask for help, which was *really* dumb. Worst of all, I threw away ten years that I could have been with the love of my life."

He spoke directly to April, focused on the girl—no—the *woman* of his dreams. "I had a letter from her that I couldn't read. That I never asked anyone else to read for me. Because I was embarrassed."

April stood, her hand over her mouth, and approached the auditorium doors. James willed her to come closer, to hear him out.

"So I left town, looking to better myself. I took special classes, so that I could finally understand what my true love wrote to me. But, by then, it was too late. The letter was gone. I never knew what it said."

Gazing at April, he remembered the hurt expression in her eyes as the older boys pointed and giggled at her son. Jimmy wanted to leap off the stage and scoop up Marcus to protect him from the barbs. The autistic boy might not be aware of them now, but one day he would and experience his share of the world's mean-spiritedness. Would Marcus revert back into his shell as a result?

Jimmy turned his focus to the crowd. "I've wasted a lot of time and energy keeping my secret. And I'm telling you now, because I saw something tonight that made me want to speak out. I saw some kids make fun of a little boy who has a disorder, who didn't ask for the challenges he has ahead. And that's not fair. That's not nice. Especially at this time of year. Like my mom said to me the other day, it's almost Christmas. Let's remember that and be considerate of other people's feelings. If everyone does their part, we can make a difference. As Pete the Cat says, he's small, but he's going to do his best."

The room was silent. Jimmy realized he should have made his

little speech *after* the performance. His own rant would be a tough act to follow. But the look of pride on April's face injected him with enough courage to carry on.

"Now, I'm not going to read this story. Because, as short as is it, we'd be here for the next half hour while I struggled through it. Luckily for all of us, I've got it memorized."

He strummed his chord again and began the first line of the poem. He could swear the mood in the auditorium was chillier than it was outside. But he could feel April's warmth and approval from the back of the room. He recited the poem just for her.

For her and Marcus.

When he got to the song, he heard rustling in the audience and a couple of nervous coughs. He kept his sights on April and her son, knowing their support would see him through to the end.

Gaining confidence, he started to let go, to do the funny voices he'd rehearsed—one for Pete and one for Santa. When he talked about the reindeer, he looked up at the ceiling while patting the wooden body of his guitar to make it sound like tiny hooves on the roof. That got a laugh. By the time he launched into a repeat of the song, he could see people tapping their toes, some mouthing the words. Even better, April was smiling.

And Marcus...

Marcus was walking up the aisle toward him, dancing as he went.

The crowd noticed the boy, some turning around to look. But instead of pointing with ridicule, they were smiling and nodding and laughing.

They weren't laughing *at* Marcus. They were joyful *with* him.

Jimmy realized he and the boy had the spectators in the palms of their hands. As the final chorus of the song began, Marcus climbed the steps of the stage and Jimmy knew he couldn't end the performance there.

"Everybody sing," he instructed and repeated the chorus again. The audience joined in, clapping in time to the rhythm, while Marcus danced up a storm.

And then, he started to sing.

One by one, the others stopped. Only Marcus remained singing—his sweet, boy's soprano voice filling the auditorium. The melody and the words, perfect.

Jimmy fell to his knees, still strumming on the guitar. Until the last line, when his eyes were so full of tears, he couldn't play anymore. He'd learned that certain autistic children were great at mimicry. They could repeat the dialogue of entire movies—but it didn't mean anything to them. He didn't know if this was the case with Marcus, but Jimmy still found it difficult to hold in the emotions that threatened to burst out of him. He viewed the boy through a watery film.

And then Marcus looked at him—*really* looked. Jimmy set his guitar down at his side and held out his arms. Marcus took one tentative step. Then another. And then ran to Jimmy.

Jimmy hugged the boy so hard he was afraid he'd crush him. Better still, Marcus hugged him right back. After a moment, Jimmy heard the clapping, the cheers. The entire audience stood, applauding.

Jimmy took Marcus by the hand, rose, and showed the boy how to bow. The people kept clapping so they kept bowing.

Two days ago, Jimmy was afraid of getting on the stage. Now, he was wondering what he could do for an encore.

In the end, he grabbed his guitar, swept up Marcus in his arms and exited down the front stairs, winking at his mother on the way by, getting a thumbs-up from Joey and feeling pats on his back from both his father and his brother.

Jimmy walked right down the center aisle to where April stood, tears in her eyes and a smile on her lips. She wrapped her arm around his waist and they made their way to the auditorium doors, the sound of applause and cheers following them out.

Jimmy left his Porsche in the parking lot so he could chauffeur April and Marcus home in her van. He had to fix everything he'd broken between them. Or, at least, as much as he could.

The vehicle was cold from being parked outside for so long, but warmed up quickly as he drove. Marcus hummed to himself in the backseat, while April sat quietly beside Jimmy, bundled in her coat like a puffed-out bird.

"Can we talk now?"

April took a deep breath. "I'm proud of you, Jimmy—standing up for people with challenges and admitting your own. That took real guts."

He supposed he should give himself a moment to bask in her praise. Because he knew there was a 'but' on her lips.

"But..."

And there it was. He cringed hearing it, knowing what was to follow. "Please, April. I can explain."

"About you and Heather...and the baby?"

Oh, God. He could barely keep the car on the road. All he could see in front of him was his world falling apart.

He started at the beginning, recapping his father's birthday party and his mother's scrapbook project. He told her about going to Billy Boy's, having a couple of drinks, and crashing at Heather's apartment to avoid driving under the influence. There, they drank a few more and he'd obviously blabbed something about the letter. He confessed he didn't remember anything happening between them, but that Heather claimed he was baby Holly's dad.

"Why didn't you tell me all this from the beginning? Why did I have to learn it from a stranger? That's what hurts the most, Jimmy. That you didn't trust me enough to confide in me."

"I trust you completely. I didn't tell you because I don't trust *Heather*." He raked his fingers across his scalp and forced himself to calm down, to lower his voice. "I wanted to verify her claim before I told *anyone*. Right after she confronted me, I bought a paternity kit. I'll have the DNA results in a few days."

The windshield wipers flapped back and forth, counting down the time like a pendulum clock. Still, April said nothing, just sat there, her gloved hands in her lap.

"Well?"

"If it turns out the child is yours, what then?"

"I'll take full responsibility for Holly. I'll support her and love her."

"Even if it means losing me?

Damn. He felt as if his heart were being ripped in two. "It would kill me to lose you again. But I'd have to do what's right for the baby."

"And Heather? Would you marry her?"

"No. That wouldn't be fair. To me or her. I can't marry another woman when I'm in love with you. Whether you return that love or not, I can't live that kind of lie and be with someone else."

April sighed—a long, slow exhale. "That's exactly what I thought you'd say."

Jimmy couldn't drive anymore. Not when April was about to

walk out of his life again. After they crossed the covered bridge, he pulled over to the side of the road and stopped the car. "So where does that leave *us?*"

"Whatever happened between you and Heather, it was before we reconnected. I haven't been entirely celibate during the past ten years, either. I can't judge you for sleeping with another woman when the two of you were single, consenting adults."

"But I don't remember sleeping with her."

"You'd been drinking, though."

He couldn't deny it. "Yes. I'd been drinking. And there are parts of that night that are a little hazy for me." Telling Heather about the letter, for instance. "I tried to drown my problems and ended up multiplying them...and I will never do that again. I won't lie and say I've gone teetotal since but, if I'm out socially or watching a football game, I may have *one* drink. Tops."

He wondered if April was thinking about her parents, about the role alcohol played in their deaths. He sure was. During the silence, the car windows fogged up, making the view beyond hazy. The outside world didn't matter to him. He knew his life hinged on April's next words.

"Jimmy, I know in the past you could be irresponsible, but that was in the way you handled school. Now I understand the reason behind it—your dyslexia. In the spring, you overindulged—a mistake, true—but you made the conscientious decision to avoid driving afterward. And when I asked you about Holly, when I suggested you choose me over her, you didn't waver. You didn't lie to appease me. With everything on the line, you're still determined to do what's right and accept your responsibilities."

April grasped his hand. "I admire that. I admire *you.*"

Really? He wished he'd told her about Heather right away and swore never to keep another secret. Happily forgiven, he leaned in for a kiss.

"Not so fast, buster. We've still got this Getalot issue to discuss."

Out of the frying pan...

Jimmy closed his eyes, inwardly kicking himself. "I'm sorry, April. I thought I was doing good. A new store means new jobs. And you'd told me you'd tried to sell the land earlier. So I put out some feelers, to see if the company was interested and what they'd offer you before getting your hopes up. But then, when I pictured the trees gone and a big parking lot beside your house, I knew it wouldn't work. I had no idea Stephen would send a man to survey—"

She held up her hand. "I get it. And it's not as if you tried to cheat me or sell the place out from under me. It was always going to be my choice, yes?"

"Yes. Absolutely." He inched closer, eager to hear her wishes. "So what do you want to do?"

"I want to keep the land. I want to have the school there and give the children a place to play. The trees and the maple syrup farm are part of that. I want to share the experience of nature with the kids, of working with it. I know they'll love the harvest as much as we did. So I need you to straighten things out with your Getalot contact. Tell him I'm not interested in selling, for any price, and that will be that."

"I'll fix it right away. I was an idiot to think you'd want to live next door to a busy store."

"We don't use the word *idiot* around here," she said, primly. "*Ass* will do in this case. Fortunately for me, you're a cute one."

Jimmy chuckled at the backhanded compliment. "I'll call Stephen and tell him to get a new contractor, too. I like working construction, but you made me realize the whole Getalot thing isn't a good fit for me. It never was. I was trying to be someone I'm not to prove a point."

"And you already proved it."

He nodded. "That means I won't be traveling as much. I can put down roots. Here in Carol Falls."

"You're staying?"

"If you'll have me."

She bowed her head in thought. When she looked up again, there was a twinkle in her eye. "You've grown up a lot since we were first together, Jimmy. I have, too. But you've always been in my heart."

She reached for the chain she wore around her neck and pulled it out of her top. Dangling from it was a simple gold band. The one he'd given her ten years ago.

"Call me sentimental, but I kept this as a good luck charm. And because I always hoped we could get married for real someday. You're the only man for me, Jimmy Frost. I love you."

Like the Grinch, his heart grew three times larger. He undid his seatbelt and slid over to her. He slipped his arms around his teenage sweetheart, his forever sweetheart, and kissed her. Kissed her until the snow stopped, until the blades of the wipers went dry and made funny squealing noises on the foggy windows...until their breaths became one.

Until Marcus started kicking the front seat, bored from the lack of movement.

"Time to get you home," Jimmy whispered in April's ear.

"Agreed. But don't think you're going to have your way with me until we're properly married. I have a reputation to uphold."

"Marrying you is the first thing I plan to do. After I get the DNA results."

"No. Before." She entwined her fingers with his. "Just like that night ten years ago, I'm taking a leap of faith. I'm trusting my heart. Because the only test that matters to me is the one you've already passed with top marks. You're a good man. A man of integrity. And I love you for it."

Jimmy thought his heart would explode. She'd just given him the best Christmas present ever. He kissed her again—her lips soft, succulent.

"So April...how do you feel about eloping to Vegas?"

EPILOGUE

Christmas morning…

Vegas wasn't in the cards. They'd made it as far as the Town Hall, with all the assorted Frosts in attendance. But it had taken some coercion. As a trade-off, Jimmy's mom made April promise to have a 'real' wedding in the spring, one she could help plan.

With Marcus doing so well, she and Jimmy had decided to add to their family right away. They'd made love every day since. Each time was a new discovery, more wonderful than the last. And, once their babies started arriving, April figured there'd be a lot more sleepless nights. But she was looking forward to all of it.

She walked over to their Christmas tree, which had finally made it into the house, and retrieved one of the packages from underneath its boughs.

"Here's your present from me," she told Jimmy, passing him the flat, rectangular gift. He peeled back the wrapping to reveal a copy of *Pete the Cat Saves Christmas*. "It was the last one they had at Book Marks." April loved the local store, owned by a father and son team—Mark Sr. and Mark Jr. "They had a run on the book after your performance."

Jimmy flipped the pages. "This is about my speed for reading, too."

"I'm going to help you with that. And, because you already have this piece memorized, I'm going to make you read it backward."

He clutched his heart as if she'd wounded him and they both laughed.

The next package Jimmy opened was from his mother. Inside was an eagle's feather, a silver dollar, an assortment of picks and two letters—the one April wrote so many years ago and a recent one from his mom.

Jimmy read the second letter out loud to April, his efforts slow but there was no problem with that. She loved hearing his voice.

Jimmy,

I found these things years ago when I replaced the flooring in your bedroom. I didn't mention the items to you sooner because, in revealing some, I'd have to reveal them all, and I wasn't sure you were ready to see the letter from April. I know how hurt you were over the annulment. I thought, when you were ready, you'd ask about it. I'm sorry now that I kept it from you.

Please forgive me if I've caused you and April extra pain. I've always prayed the two of you would find each other again and I consider myself a lucky woman to have such a wonderful daughter-in-law...once more.

Your loving mother.

P.S. I look forward to seeing you all for Christmas dinner. Your father and I are excited about getting to know our new grandson.

Jimmy unfolded April's letter and read it next, clutching it to his chest afterward. "I think I'll frame this one."

"I'm going to have to start calling you Mr. Romance, if you keep talking pretty to me like that."

"Best to reserve judgment until you open the gift I got you. It might not seem very romantic at first glance." He passed her a thick envelope. Inside was money. More bills than she'd ever seen in her life.

But *money?* For *Christmas?*

"So we can make your dreams for this farm come true," he explained. "To turn this place into a school."

Several Benjamin Franklin's peeked out at her from the stack. "But where did you get all this cash?"

"I sold my car. To the mayor."

"You loved that car."

"Not really." He shrugged. "It wasn't me. It was all about the person I was trying to be. What I care about now is being a good husband and father."

"And a musician?"

"I've thought about that. When I was last in the Hawk & Hound Pub, I noticed they had an advertisement looking for entertainment on Friday nights—someone to sing and play guitar. I'll apply for that, and I'll keep doing private contracting. I hear the Belmonts' house could use a new roof. Garret wants to expand, too. I thought we could enter into the same arrangement as your grandfather had years ago and supply Frost Farms with maple sap."

"The Frost brothers in business together. Who'd have *thunk* it?"

"Even with all those options, I doubt I'll make as much money as I did from Getalot, but it'll be fun and I can stick close to home. I've already spent too many nights of my life away from you."

She plunked herself down on his lap and kissed him. "I know you're going to be the very best at all of those things, James."

"About that name. I really don't feel like a James, you know. It's kind of pretentious, don't you think?"

"Darn. I just got used to it. Should I go back to calling you Jimmy?"

"How 'bout...*Jim*. Straightforward, solid, reliable. Exactly the kind of man I want to be for you and Marcus...and any other little ones that come our way."

Could she possibly adore him more? She kissed him again, wanting to take him right back to the warm bed they'd just left.

"I want to fill the house with children, April. And, if you're willing, I'd like to start with baby Holly."

She sat back and eyed him closely. "After all you've been through with Heather, you're still willing to raise her child?"

"Only if her real father doesn't show up. With the extra babysitting we've done in the last couple of weeks, I confess, I've become really attached to her."

"Me, too. I'd love to adopt Holly."

Marcus scampered over with the computer tablet they'd purchased for him as an early Christmas present, so he could communicate. He still didn't speak, but he could sing up a storm and pluck out letters on the keyboard like nobody's business. Marcus climbed up on Jim's knee, as well, to show the adults what he'd typed on the tablet's screen.

'Me, too.'

Not to be outdone, Bandit the cat jumped on the chair and made himself comfortable on Jim's shoulder, purring loudly. Friends at last.

"So we're all in agreement," he said, revealing a small box from the chest pocket of his shirt. "One more gift."

She opened the box to discover a golden heart pendant, engraved with the letters J. F. & A. R., exactly the way he'd carved their initials into the dear, old maple tree.

"Since you're wearing your ring again, I figured you needed a new lucky charm for your chain. Do you like it?"

"I love it. And *you*," she said, as a knock sounded on the front door.

He scrambled out of his chair and went to answer it. When he opened the door, there was no one there. Jim heard an engine and saw an old car puttering down the road.

He was about to close the door when he noticed a package on the mat. He picked it up and brought it inside.

"Who's that from?" April asked.

"Heather, I think."

"Should we call the bomb squad?"

Jim held the package to his ear. "It isn't ticking." He carried it over to the chair and opened it so everyone could see the contents—a pair of hand-knitted kids' mittens, a matching scarf, a twenty dollar bill and a third note.

Jim figured it was a very good thing he'd learned to read. He was getting lots of practice today. April peered at the note over his shoulder.

James,

I'm so sorry for all the trouble I caused you. Please accept these gifts for your new son as a peace offering.

By now, I'm sure you've received the results from the DNA test and you know you're not Holly's father. There's been some talk around town you might be willing to adopt her anyway. If you feel the slightest hesitation in doing so because of me, please know this—I am not the baby's mother.

I was at Frosty Frolics the night Holly was found—but I didn't see who left her in the manger. It certainly wasn't me. I first learned about her the following day, like most people in town. It wasn't until you came into Kate's, driving up in your expensive car, that I saw a chance to use you and your family's good name. I thought if I could convince you to marry me, Child Protective Services would let Charlotte come home.

Realizing it had been about nine months since we met, I quickly planned a way to trap you. That's why I told you Holly was yours, and let you think we'd been intimate. All lies. We never touched that night. In any way. Please believe me about that.

And the fact that I did fall for you. How could I not? You gave me more respect than I give myself.

You're a remarkable man, James, and I wish I hadn't thrown away what could have been a wonderful friendship between us. I know it was wrong and cruel to involve you, when all you've been is kind and decent to me. And I truly regret my attempts to come between you and April. I can only say, I was desperate and I hope you will find it in your heart to forgive me.

I'm enclosing $20, my first step toward repaying what you loaned me. (Yes, I'm considering it a loan.) I'm leaving town today, so you don't have to worry about running into me by chance, which I know would be awkward for you and your new family.

All the best to you and yours,
Heather.

April dabbed her nose with a tissue. "I want to forgive her. I really do. But it's going to take time."

With all that Heather had done to disrupt his life, Jim agreed.

During the past weeks, he'd come close to telling the police that Heather was the baby's mother. He'd always stopped himself. Mostly because he didn't want to see Heather face criminal charges. Not when she was fighting to regain custody of Charlotte. Now he was glad he'd stayed silent on the matter.

Ironic that Holly's mother had abandoned her, while Heather was willing to risk anything to reclaim her child. The two stories tied together and had almost bound him up in the process.

"Too bad she left town," he said. "I would have liked to help her get her daughter back." Reuniting the two would have gone a long way to bring him closure.

"That's so like you." April wove her fingers through his hair. "I hope, one day, Heather finds a good man like I have."

"Now who's talking pretty?"

After another kiss, April let out a long, contented sigh, and then turned serious. "So...we still don't know who Holly's parents are."

"No. But we do know she'll have a loving family with us, should she need it."

According to his sister, the police continued to investigate the mystery. Jim was proud Joey wore a badge. He'd learned she was a tenacious officer and worked hard for the community. If anyone could find Holly's parents, it was Joey.

Jim kicked back, counting his own good fortunes, while he hugged his new wife and son. He caught sight of the Christmas tree topper, the angel gazing down at them, and he felt right and truly

blessed to finally be...
    Home for Christmas.

THE MYSTERY OF THE ABANDONED BABY CONCLUDES WITH...
THE HOLLY & THE IVY (BOOK THREE)
Joey's story
by Brenda M. Collins

AND DON'T MISS THE START OF IT ALL...
WHAT CHILD IS THIS (BOOK ONE)
Garret's story
by C. J. Carmichael

In response to readers' requests,
the FROST FAMILY series
continues with...
MORE THAN A FEELING (BOOK FOUR)
by C. J. Carmichael

If you enjoyed ***HOME FOR CHRISTMAS***,
please help other readers find it
by recommending it to friends
or writing a review.

About Roxy Boroughs

Before turning her attention to fiction, Roxy appeared in numerous TV commercials and movies.

In addition to **HOME FOR CHRISTMAS**, she's also published the romantic comedy **CRAZY FOR COWBOY** and a sweet romance anthology called **STORIES OF CHANCE ROMANCE** with Brenda M. Collins, as well as two romantic suspense titles. Check them all out on her Amazon Page.

Visit Roxy at www.roxyboroughs.com.

www.ingramcontent.com/pod-product-compliance
Lightning Source LLC
Chambersburg PA
CBHW060130260626
47160CB00005B/2057